Options

Robert Sheckley's first science fiction and fantasy stories were published in 1951 while he was still at the University of New York. In 1952, after working for six months as an X-ray technician in an aircraft plant, he became a full-time writer. His books include *Immortality Inc*, *Journey Beyond Tomorrow*, *Mindswap*, *The People Trap* and *The Same to You Doubled.*

Born in 1928, Mr Sheckley wa
with his wife in New York and
not on a trip, he is always plan

Previously published by Robert Sheckley in Pan

The People Trap
Mindswap
The Same to You Doubled

Robert Sheckley

Options

Pan Books London and Sydney

First British edition published 1977 by
Pan Books Ltd, Cavaye Place, London SW10 9PG

ISBN 0 330 24885 5
Printed and bound in Great Britain by
Hunt Barnard Printing Ltd, Aylesbury, Bucks

To Abby
with love and gratitude

Mind is the Buddha, while the cessation of conceptual thought is the Way. Once you stop arousing concepts and thinking in terms of existence and non-existence, long and short, other and self, active and passive, and suchlike, you will find that your mind is intrinsically the Buddha, that the Buddha is intrinsically Mind, and that Mind resembles a void.

The Zen Teaching of Huang Po.

Part One

NOTICE

The rules of normalcy will be temporarily suspended while new rules are being drawn. The new rules may not be the same as the old rules. No hints can be given concerning the new rules.

The best thing to do might be to avoid conflict situations, spend the rest of the day in bed, cool out.

Or, if that sounds boring, I could take you for a ride.

1 Use of 'Simple Premises' Termed Misleading

Tom Mishkin was tooling along through the Lesser Magellanic Cloud at a low multiple of the speed of light, moving along smartly but not really pushing it. His ship, the *Intrepid III*, was loaded with frozen South African lobster tails, tennis shoes, air conditioners, malted milk makers, and other general stores, bound for the settlement on Dora V. Mishkin was catnapping in a big command chair, lulled by the light patterns rippling across the control board and by the quiet snap and crackle of the circuit breakers. He was thinking of a new apartment he planned to buy in the town of Perth Amboy-bas-mer, ten miles due east of Sandy Hook. You could get a little peace and quiet in the suburbs, although the problem of commuting by submarine . . .

One of the snaps turned into a clank.

Mishkin sat upright, his pilot's ear always attuned for the Malfunction That Could Not Happen but frequently did.

Clank, clank, clank, crunch.

Yes. It had happened.

Mishkin groaned – that special pilot's groan compounded of foreknowledge, fatalism, and heartburn. He could hear bad things happening deep in the guts of the ship. The Malfunction Telltale (supposedly for external impingement only) went violet, then red, then purple, then black. The ship's computer awoke from its dogmatic slumber long enough to growl, 'Malfunction, malfunction, malfunction.'

'Thanks, I already got the idea,' Mishkin said. 'Where is it and what is it?'

'Malfunction in Part L-1223A. Catalogue name: Port Side Crossover Lock Valve Assembly and Retainer Ring. Proximate cause of malfunction: 8 (eight) sheered bolts plus spiral fracture in retainer ring housing. Intermediate cause: angular pressure on aforesaid parts resulted in molecular changes in metal composition of aforementioned parts, resulting in the condition known as metal fatigue.'

'Yeah. But why?' Mishkin asked.

'Conjecture as to primary cause: various bolts in said assembly torqued to unacceptable pressures, thus reducing the assembly's life to 84.3 hours rather than the 195.441 working years called for in the specifications.'

'Very nice,' Mishkin said. 'What's happening now?'

'I have cut out the unit and shut down the main drive.'

'Up space creek without a paddle,' Mishkin commented. 'Can I use the main drive at all, just long enough to get to the nearest Ship Service Centre?'

'Negative. Use of aforementioned malfunctioned Part would cause immediate and cumulative distortions in other parts of Main Drive, resulting in total disablement, implosion, and death, and a permanent black mark on your service record. You would also be billed for a new spaceship.'

'Well, I certainly don't want any black marks on my record,' Mishkin said. 'What should I do?'

'Your only feasible option is to remove and replace the

malfunctioned Part. Caches of spare parts have been established on various uninhabited planets to cover such a necessity. The planet nearest to your present coordinates is Harmonia II, 68 hours from here by secondary drive.'

'That sounds simple enough,' Mishkin said.

'It is, theoretically.'

'But practically?'

'There are always complications.'

'Such as?'

'If we knew that,' the computer told him, 'the complications wouldn't be very complicated, would they?'

'I suppose not,' Mishkin said. 'All right, cut a course and let's get going.'

'To hear is to obey,' the computer said.

USE OF 'MULTIPLE PREMISES' TERMED CONFUSING

In an exclusive press interview yesterday, Professor David Hume of Harvard declared that sequence did not imply causality. When asked to amplify, he pointed out that sequence is merely additive, not generative.

We asked Dr Emmanuel Kant for his opinion on this statement. Professor Kant, in his Cal Tech study, looked badly shaken. 'This,' he said, 'has awakened me from my dogmatic slumber.'

2 The Mad Synaesthesiast Strikes

Mishkin leaned back in the chair and closed his eyes. That was bad: derangement of various sense ratios, ideas of reference, hot flashes. He opened his eyes. That was not so good either. He reached for the Turn-off Bottle. It had a label that read, IF THE TRIP GOES BAD, DRINK THIS. He drank it, then noticed a label on the other side of the bottle that read, IF THE TRIP GOES BAD, DO *NOT* DRINK THIS.

One of the radios was moaning softly to itself, 'Oh, God, I'll be killed. I just know I'll be killed. Why did I ever go on this crazy trip? It wasn't good enough for me to just sit in the window at the Hallicrafters and dig the scene. No, I had to get active about it and where in hell am I now?'

Mishkin had no time for the radio. He had problems of his own. At least he assumed that they were his own. It was difficult to be sure.

He found that he had only imagined opening his eyes. Therefore he opened his eyes. But had he really? He considered opening his eyes again, in case he had only imagined it again, but stopped himself, thus avoiding a really nasty form of infinite regression.

The radio was babbling again: 'God, I don't know where I'm going. But if I knew where I was going I wouldn't go there. But not knowing where I'm going, I don't know how not to go there because I don't know where I'm going. Damn it, this isn't the way it's supposed to be. They told me it would be fun.'

Mishkin quickly drank the contents of the Turn-off Bottle. It couldn't get much worse he decided, which showed how much he knew.

Firmness seemed called for. Mishkin sat up straight in his chair. He said, 'Now hear this. We will proceed to act on the premise that we all are what we seem to be at this moment and that we will remain this way indefinitely. That is an order. Is it understood?'

The turntable said, 'Everything's going to goddamn hell

and he's giving orders, yet. What's with you, Jack, you think this is a goddamned *submarine* or something?'

'We must all pull together,' Mishkin said, 'else we shall all be pulled apart.'

'Platitudes, yet,' the armchair said. 'We could all be killed and he's spouting platitudes.'

Mishkin shuddered and drank the contents of the Turn-on Bottle, then put it down quickly before the bottle had a chance to drink him. Bottles had been known to do that; you could never tell when it was role-reversal time.

'Now I shall land this ship,' Mishkin said.

'It's a dreary premise,' the control board said. 'But go ahead and play games if you want to.'

'Shut up,' Mishkin said. 'You're a control board.'

'What would you say if I told you that I am a middle-aged psychiatrist from New York City and that your act of labelling me a control board – by which you mean a *to-be-controlled board* – or *bored* – shows where your head is at, powerstrugglewise?'

Mishkin decided to drink the contents of the Turn-on Bottle. He was in enough trouble as it was. With an enormous effort he blew his nose. Lights flashed.

A man in a blue uniform came through the baggage room and said, 'All tickets, please.' Mishkin gave him his ticket, which the man punched.

Mishkin punched a button, which took it like a man. There were groans and squeaks. Was he coming down?

3 New 'Plausibility Generator' said to Cure Schizophrenia

The cache on Harmonia was a large brightly lighted structure, all stainless steel and glass, looking irrevocably like a Miami Beach supermarket. Mishkin drove his spaceship in, turned off the engine, and put the key in his pocket. He walked down the gleaming aisles past shelves loaded with trays of transistors, six-pacs of silicones, vapour recovery systems, chuck roasts, freezer-pacs of glycol brine, baby spectrometers, spark plugs, coaxial loudspeakers, tuner modules, foil-sealed vitamin B_6 capsules, and nearly everything else that the far-travelling tripper of inner/outer space might require.

He came to the central communications panel. There he asked for Part L-1223A.

He waited. Minutes passed.

'Hey!' Mishkin called out. 'What happened? What's up?'

'Terribly sorry,' the control panel replied. 'I'm afraid I was woolgathering. I've been having rather a trying time of it.'

'What's been the matter?' Mishkin asked.

'Difficulties, many difficulties,' the panel said. 'Really, you can have no idea. My head is positively swimming. I speak figuratively, of course.'

'You talk funny for a control panel,' Mishkin said, suspiciously.

'These days control panels come equipped with personalities. It makes us seem less *inhuman*, if you know what I mean.'

'So what's been going wrong around here?' Mishkin asked.

'Well, I suppose a lot of it is *me*,' the control panel said. 'You see, when you equip a computer with a personality, well, it's like giving him the ability to *feel*. And if we can *feel* then you can't expect us to do the old, soulless thing any more. I mean to say, my personality makes it impossible for me to do a robot-like job, even though essentially I *am* a robot and the job I have to do *should* be done in essentially a robot-like fashion. But I can't do that, I'm absentminded, I have my bad days, my moods . . . Does that make any sense to you?'

'Of course it does,' Mishkin said. 'Now, what about that part?'

'It isn't inside here. It's outside.'

'Where outside?'

'About fifteen miles away, or possibly twenty.'

'But what is it doing outside?'

'Well, originally we had all the parts stockpiled here inside the cache. All very logical and convenient. Perhaps it was too simple for the human mind to endure, for all of a sudden some humans got to thinking, "What would happen if a disabled ship crashed *right on top of the cache*?" That freaked everybody out, so the problem was fed to a computer, and the answer came up, "Decentralize!" The engineers and planners nodded and said, "Decentralize, *of course*, why didn't *we* think of that?" So orders were cut and work teams came out and stuck parts all over the area. And then everybody sat back and said, "Well, *that's* OK now." And then the trouble *really* began.'

'What sort of trouble?' Mishkin asked.

'Well, humans had to leave the cache and go out on to the surface of Harmonia in order to get what they needed. And that meant danger. Alien planets are dangerous, you know, because alien things happen on them, and one does not know how to respond, and by the time one figures out what the situation is and how to deal with it, it has already come and gone and maybe killed you.'

'What sort of alien things?' Mishkin asked.

'I am not allowed to mention specifics,' the computer said. 'If I did, it would all get much trickier.'

'Why?'

'Successful adaptation to alien dangers requires the broad-spectrum ability to recognize what constitutes danger and what does not. If I were to mention only one or two possibilities you would become overconditioned – the so-called tunnel effect – thus limiting your perceptions of other risk situations. Besides, it isn't necessary.'

'Why not?'

'Because provision has been made. You will be accompanied outside by a SPER robot. If we have one in stock. There was a mix-up in the last shipment . . .'

The control panel became silent. Mishkin said, 'What . . .'

'*Please*,' said the panel, 'I'm checking the inventory.'

Mishkin waited. In a few moments the panel said, 'Yes, we do have a SPER robot in stock. It came in the last shipment. It would have been pretty *gross* if that had been missing, too.'

'What is this robot?' Mishkin asked. 'What is it supposed to do?'

'The initials stand for Special Purpose Environmental Response robot. These machines are programmed to respond to the conditions of a specific alien world. They detect whatever might constitute noxious stimuli to a human, warn him, defend him, and suggest appropriate counter-measures. With a SPER robot you'll be as safe as if you were back in New York.'

'Thanks a lot,' Mishkin said.

4 Chicken Little Claims Personification most Common Sign of Impaired Sense Ratios

The SPER robot was short and rectangular. His lacquered, scarlet case was most attractive. He walked on four spindly limbs and had four more on the upper part of his control case. He resembled a tarantula disguised as a robot.

He said to Mishkin. 'OK, sonny, let's get cracking.'

'Will it be very dangerous?' Mishkin asked.

'Piece of cake. I could do it blindfolded.'

'What should I watch out for?'

'I'll let you know.'

Mishkin shrugged and followed the robot past the check-out counter and through the swinging doors out on to the surface of Harmonia. He figured that the robot knew what he was doing. But Mishkin was wrong. His lack of knowledge was monstrous, ineluctable, and strangely touching. Perhaps only a virgin mounted on a unicorn could have been quite so dumb as Mishkin.

(Of course, his robot buddy was not exactly the last word in smart, either. Add his ignorance to Mishkin's and you get a really big negative number equal to the cases of pleurisy since the beginning of the second Peloponnesian War.)

Jam, hot cross buns, fellatio, the colour of lips, these were on his mind as Mishkin stepped tumulously on to the dubious surface of Harmonia.

'How long do the hallucinations continue?' Mishkin asked.

'Why ask me?' said the kindly chef with the battered harmonica. 'I, too, am an hallucination.'

'How can I tell which things are real and which are not?'

'Try litmus paper,' advised Chuang-tzu.

'The whole deal is this,' said the robot. 'You gotta do exactly like I say – otherwise you're real dead in a hurry. Got it?'

'Got it,' said Mishkin. They were strolling a purple plain. The wind was from the east at five miles an hour, and one could hear the electronic sound of birds.

'When I tell you to git down,' the robot went on, 'you gotta hit the deck fast. There'll be no time for blinking and stumbling. I just hope that your reflexes are in good shape.'

'I thought you said it wasn't dangerous here,' Mishkin said.

'So, big deal, you've caught me in a contradiction,' the robot sneered. 'Maybe I had my reasons for lying to you.'

'What were they?'

'Maybe I've got my reasons for not telling you,' the robot said. 'Just listen to what I say now. *Hit it!*'

Mishkin, too, had heard the faint, high-pitched drone. He threw himself on the grass, bruising his nose in his eagerness to comply. He could see the robot swivelling, two blasters in his metal hands.

'What is it?' Mishkin asked.

'Mating call of the six-legged proto-Brontostegosaurus. When the durned critters are in heat, they'll try to make it with anything.'

'Can't they see that I am not an appropriate object for their affections?'

'Sure, but it takes a few minutes for the message to get through to their brains, since the proto-B is not exactly anyone's idea of bright. And in the meantime, you got twenty-three tons of inflamed critter squatting on your head.'

'So where is it?' Mishkin asked.

'It's coming,' the robot said grimly, twirling the blasters by their trigger guards.

The drone increased in volume and amplitude. Then Mishkin saw something that looked like a butterfly with a six-foot wingspan come fluttering past, droning merrily. It ignored them and went off stage left.

'What was that?' Mishkin asked.

'It sure as hell looked like a butterfly with a six-foot wingspan,' the robot said.

'That's what I thought. But you said . . .'

'Yes, yes, yes,' the robot said testily. 'It's obvious enough what happened. That butterfly critter has learned how to imitate the mating cry of the proto-B. Mimicry is a commonplace phenomenon throughout the galaxy.'

'Commonplace? It took *you* by surprise.'

'What's so surprising about that? It was the first time I ever encountered that butterfly critter.'

'You should have known about it,' Mishkin said.

'Wrong. I'm programmed only to detect and cope with situations and things that'll be dangerous to humans. That big old flapper couldn't hurt you unless you tried to swallow it, so naturally enough I've got nothing on it in my memory files. You gotta realize that I'm not a goddamned encyclopedia. I deal strictly with dangerous stuff, not with every damned thing that walks or swims or flies or crawls or burrows or however it happens to get around. You get my meaning, son?'

'I get it,' Mishkin said. 'I suppose you know what you're doing.'

'That's what I happen to have been built for,' the robot said. 'C'mon, let's get on with this promenade.'

5 The Prepared Statement

'I have been having mental difficulties for some time now. I get these ideas, these images. But I don't know what is real and what is not. Sometimes I think that I've eaten and then I find that I have not. Sometimes I think that I have lived and then I find that I have not. I cannot remember why I am here or what crime I stand accused of. Whatever it is, I am sure that I am innocent. I am sure that I am innocent, no matter what I have done.'

Mishkin looked up hopefully but found that the jury had recessed, the judge had recessed, the world had recessed, and a bored guard was thumbing through an old issue of *Rolling Stone.*

Mishkin came to a sudden stop.

'What is it?' the robot asked.

'I see something up ahead.'

'Big deal,' the robot sneered. 'I see plenty of things up ahead. I *always* see plenty of things up ahead. Christ, *everybody always* sees plenty of things up ahead.'

'This thing up ahead seems to be an animal.'

'What's so impressive about that?'

The thing that Mishkin saw up ahead was roughly the size and shape of a tiger but with a shorter tail and bigger feet. It was coloured a dappled chocolate with brilliant orange stripes. It looked like a mean, hungry, and unscrupulous hallucination.

'It looks dangerous,' Mishkin said.

'That shows how much you know about it,' the robot told him. 'That there critter is a pachynert, which is an herbivorous beast with a disposition like a cow's, only more timid.'

'But the teeth.'

'Don't let the teeth fake you out.'

'Mimicry?'

'That's it, ace. Now git ahold of yourself and let's move out.'

They continued across the purple plain. The robot, not even bothering to draw his blasters, was whistling 'Elmer's Tune'. Mishkin, walking two steps behind him, was humming 'Valse Triste'.

The pachynert turned towards them and stared with eyes the colour of coagulated yak's blood. He yawned, revealing incisors like Turkish scimitars. He stretched, showing a smooth ripple of muscle down either flank like sluggish octopi grappling beneath a thin sheet of plastic.

'You're sure he's herbivorous?' Mishkin asked.

'Nothing but grass and dandelions,' the robot said. 'Although they do appreciate an occasional turnip.'

'He looks pretty mean.'

'Nature is capable of myriad disguises.'

Man and robot came closer to the beast. The pachynert laid back his ears. His tail stood out stiff and straight and high, like the indicator of a dial calibrated for trouble. He stretched out claws like the cruel, curved tines of the devil's pitchfork. He snarled – a sound that prompted several peripatetic trees to close down their branches, pull up their roots, and make for quieter territory on the north forty.

'Nature is overdoing it,' Mishkin said. 'I could swear that that critter is about to attack us.'

'Nature exaggerates,' the robot said. 'That is the nature of nature.'

They were within ten yards of the pachynert, which stood utterly still and gave an excellent imitation of a deadly animal about to charge in a berserk manner and maim and kill any human in sight – and maybe a robot and a couple of trees, too, just for the hell of it.

Mishkin stopped. 'Now, look,' he said, 'there's something wrong about all this. I think...'

'You think too much,' the robot said, in a tight, hard voice. 'For God's sake, get hold of yourself, man. I am a SPER robot especially trained for this work, and I give you my word that that pitiful cow in tiger's clothing . . .'

Just then the pachynert charged. One moment it was standing still, the next moment it had burst into a furious rush, claws and teeth gleaming golden in the afternoon glare of the saffron Harmonia sun and its dull, mysterious, little red companion. The beast came with a maximum of verisimilitude, just like a hungry, feral, omnivorous beast who doesn't care what it goes up against, especially if the target is of a manageable size and hasn't got much in the way of claws and teeth.

'Shoo, pachynert, shoo!' the robot called out in an unconvincing voice.

'Hit the deck!' shouted Mishkin.

'Aaaaagggrrrh!' roared the pachynert.

6

'Tom, are you all right?'

Mishkin blinked. 'I'm fine.'

'You don't look fine.'

Mishkin giggled : that was a very funny remark.

'What's so funny?'

'You're funny. I can't even see you, and that's funny.'

'Drink this.'

'What is it?'

'Nothing. Just drink it.'

'Drink nothing and you turn into nothing!' Mishkin roared. With a supreme effort he opened his eyes. He couldn't see anything. He forced himself to see things. Now what? What was the rule? Yes! *Reality is achieved by the indefinite enumeration of objects.* Therefore: bed table, fluorescent light, incandescent light, stove, chest, bookcase, typewriter, window, tiles, glass, bottle of milk, coffee mug, guitar, ice bucket, friend, garbage bag . . . *et cetera.*

'I have achieved reality,' Mishkin said, with quiet pride. 'I'm going to be all right now.'

'What is reality?'

'One of the many possible illusions.'

Mishkin burst into tears. He had wanted an exclusive reality. This was terrible, this was worse than before. Now anything . . .

'This can't be happening,' he thought. But there was the pachynert, like a dubious proof of its own reality, coming at him in an extremely plausible whirlwind of claws and teeth. Mishkin accepted the gambit. He threw himself to one side and the beast swept past him.

'Shoot!' Mishkin screamed, getting into the spirit of the thing.

'I am not supposed to kill herbivorous animals,' the robot said. But there was little conviction in his voice.

The pachynert had wheeled around and was coming again, drooling. Mishkin jumped to the right, then to the left. The pachynert followed like his shadow. The massive jaws opened. Mishkin closed his eyes.

He felt a burst of heat on his face. He heard a snarl, a grunt, and the sound of something heavy falling.

He opened his eyes. The robot had finally brought himself to fire and had dropped the beast neatly at Mishkin's feet.

'Herbivorous,' Mishkin said, bitterly.

'There is such a thing as behavioural mimicry, you know. In actual cases the imitative behaviour is carried to the point of living like the model predator, even to the point of eating flesh; which, to a herbivore, is both repugnant and indigestible.'

'Do you believe any of that?'

'No,' the robot said, miserably. 'But I don't understand how that creature could have been left out of my memory files. This planet was under continual survey for ten years before a cache was established here. Nothing the size of that beast could have escaped the probes. It is no exaggeration to say that, dangerwise, Darbis IV is as well known as Earth itself.'

'Wait a minute,' Mishkin said. 'What planet did you say this was?'

'Darbis IV, the planet for which I was programmed.'

'This is not Darbis IV,' Mishkin said. He felt sick, dull, doomed. 'This planet is called Harmonia. They sent you to the wrong planet.'

7

Tired of the flow? Sick of unity?

Then avail yourself of

DIAL-AN-INTERRUPTION SERVICE!

Choose from our full line of Pauses, Beats, Breaks, Blackouts.

The robot chuckled – an insincere sound. 'I'm afraid you're in a bit of a funk. Temporary aphasic hysteria is my diagnosis, though God knows, I'm no doctor. The strain, I suppose . . .'

Mishkin shook his head. 'Figure it out for yourself. You've been wrong several times about the dangers here. Grossly wrong. Impossibly wrong.'

'It *is* odd,' the robot said. 'I can't think of a ready explanation.'

'I can. They've been screwing up the shipments ever since they established this cache. They simply screwed up on you. You were supposed to go to Darbis IV. But they sent you to Harmonia.'

'I'm thinking,' said the robot.

'Do that,' Mishkin said.

'I have thought,' the robot said. 'We SPER robots are noted for the speed of our synaptic responses.'

'Bully for you,' Mishkin said. 'What conclusion have you reached?'

'I think that, weighing all the available evidence, your hypothesis is the most apparently probable. I do indeed seem to have been dispatched to the wrong planet. And that, of course, presents us with a definite problem.'

'And that means we have to do some hard thinking.'

'Most assuredly. But let me point out that a creature of unknown disposition and appetites is presently approaching us.'

Mishkin nodded absently. Events were moving along too fast, and he needed a plan. To save his life he had to think, even if it cost him his life.

The robot was programmed for Darbis IV. Mishkin was programmed for Earth. And here they both were on Harmonia like two blind men in a boiler room. The most reasonable course of action for Mishkin was to go back to the cache. There he could relay the information to Earth and wait until either a replacement part or a replacement robot, or both, were shipped to Harmonia. That, however, could take months, or even years. And the part he wanted was only a few miles away.

Still, turning back was the safest course of action.

But then Mishkin thought of the conquistadors in the New World, cutting their way through endless jungle, meeting the unknown and subduing it. Was he so much less a man than they? Had the unknown changed in any fundamental way since the Phoenicians took their ships beyond the Pillars of Hercules?

He would never be able to face himself if he turned back now and acknowledged himself less of a man than Hanno, Cortez, Pizarro, and all of the other nuts.

On the other hand, if he went on and failed he would have no self to acknowledge.

What he really wanted to do, he decided, was to go on and succeed but not if it meant getting killed.

All in all, it was an interesting problem and one that a man might fruitfully contemplate for quite some time. A few weeks' thought might well bring him the correct answer and spare him untold . . .

'The creature is approaching rather rapidly,' the robot said.

'Well? Shoot it.'

'Maybe it's harmless.'

'Let's shoot first and think about all of that later.'

'Shooting is not an appropriate response to all dangerous situations,' the robot said.

'It is on Earth.'

'It's not on Darbis IV,' the robot said. 'There, immobility is a much safer stratagem.'

'The question is,' Mishkin said, 'whether this place is more like Earth or like Darbis.'

'If we knew that,' the robot said, 'we'd really know something.'

The new menace appeared to be a worm some twenty feet long, coloured orange, with black bands around each of its segments. The worm had five heads arranged in a cluster at one end. Each head had a single multifaceted eye and a deep, toothless, moist green mouth.

'Anything that big has got to be dangerous,' Mishkin said.

'Not on Darbis,' the robot told him. 'There, the bigger they come, the nicer they are. It's the little bastards you have to watch out for.'

'What do you suggest we do now?' Mishkin asked.

'Beats the hell out of me,' the robot said.

The worm came to within ten feet of them. The mouths opened.

'Shoot!' Mishkin said.

The robot raised his blasters and fired directly at the worm's uplifted thorax. Several of the worm's heads blinked and looked annoyed. No other change could be observed. The robot lifted his blasters again, but Mishkin told him to stop.

'That's not going to do it,' he said. 'What else do you have in mind?'

'Immobility.'

'To hell with that, I think we should run like crazy.'

'No time,' the robot said. 'Freeze!'

Mishkin forced himself to stand perfectly still as the worm's heads approached him. He shut his eyes tightly and listened to the following conversation:

'Let's eat him, huh, Vince?'

'Shaddup, Eddie, we ate a whole ormitung last night, you wanna give us indigestion?'

'I'm still hungry.'

'So am I.'

'Me too.'

Mishkin opened his eyes and saw that the worm's five heads were talking to each other. The one named Vince was in the middle and was noticeably larger than the other heads. Vince was saying, 'You guys make me sick, you and your eating! Just when I get our body in shape after working out at the gym all month, you wanna go put a belly on us and I say nix to that.'

One of the heads snivelled, 'We can eat anything we want whenever we want. Our Poppa, God rest his soul, said it was all of ours body and we was to share it equally.'

'Poppa also said that I was to look after you kids,' Vince said, 'because between you all you ain't got enough brains to climb a tree. And besides, Poppa never ate strangers.'

'That's true.' The head turned towards Mishkin. 'I'm Eddie.'

The other heads also turned. 'I'm Lucco.'

'I'm Joe.'

'I'm Chico. And that's Vince. OK, Vince, we're gonna eat him now 'cause there's four of us and we're tired of you always giving orders just because you're oldest, and from now on we're going to do exactly what the hell we want to do and if you don't like it you can damned well lump it. OK, Vince?'

'Shaddap!' Vince bellowed. 'If anyone does any eating around here it's going to be me.'

'But how about us?' Chico whined. 'Poppa said . . .'

'Anything I eat will be for all of you,' Vince said.

'But we won't be able to *taste* anything unless we eat for ourselves,' Eddie said.

'Tough,' Vince sneered. 'I'll do the tasting for all of us.'

Mishkin ventured to speak. 'Excuse me, Vince . . .'

'Mr Pagliotelli to you,' Vince said.

'I just wanted to point out that I am a form of intelligent life, and where I come from one intelligent creature does not eat another intelligent creature except under really exceptional circumstances.'

'You trying to teach me manners?' Vince said. 'I gotta good mind to break your back for making a remark like that. Besides, you attacked me first.'

'That was before I knew you were intelligent.'

'You trying to put me on?' Vince said. 'Me, intelligent? I never even finished high school! Ever since Poppa died I've had to work twelve hours a day in the sheet metal shop just to keep the kids in orlotans. But at least I'm smart enough to know that I ain't smart.'

'You sound pretty smart to me,' Mishkin said smarmily.

'Oh, sure, I got a certain native shrewdness. I'm maybe as smart as any other uneducated Wop worm. But educationwise . . .'

'Formal education is frequently overrated,' Mishkin pointed out.

'Don't I know it,' Vince said. 'But how else are you going to get along in the world?'

'It's tough,' Mishkin admitted.

'You'll laugh at me when I tell you this, but what I really always wanted to do was study the violin. Isn't that funny?'

'Not at all,' Mishkin said.

'Can you imagine me, big stupid Vince Pagliotelli, playing stuff from *Aïda* on a goddamned *fiddle*?'

'Why not?' Mishkin said. 'I'm sure you have a talent.'

'The way I see it,' Vince said, 'I had a dream. Then life came along full-freighted with responsibilities, and I exchanged the insubstantial gossamer fabric of vision for the coarse grey cloth of – of—'

'Bread?' Mishkin suggested.

'Duty?' asked Chico.

'Responsibility?' asked the robot.

'Naw, none of them's quite it,' said Vince. 'An uneducated dumbell like me oughtn't to fool around with parallel constructions.'

'Perhaps you could change the key terms,' the robot suggested. 'Try "gossamer fabric of poesy for the coarse grey cloth of the mundane".'

Vince glared at the robot, then asked Mishkin, 'Who's your wise-guy buddy?'

'He's a SPER robot,' Mishkin said. 'But he's on the wrong planet.'

'Well, tell him to watch his mouth. I don't let no goddamned robot talk to me that way.'

'Sorry about that,' the robot said briskly.

'Forget it. I guess I ain't going to eat either of you. But if you want some advice you'll watch your step around here. Not everyone is as basically distractable, good-hearted, and childlike as I am. Other persons in this forest would as soon eat you as look at you. They'd *rather* eat you, frankly, because you don't neither of you look so good to look at.'

'What sort of things should we look out for, specifically?' Mishkin asked.

'Everything, specifically,' Vince replied.

8

Mishkin and the robot thanked the good-natured Wop worm and nodded politely to his ill-mannered brothers. They moved on through the forest, for now there seemed no other way to go. Slowly they marched, and then more rapidly, and each sensed at his footsteps the sour breath and sodden cough of old mortality shuffling along behind them as usual. The robot commented on this, but Mishkin was too preoccupied to answer.

They passed huge rough trees that peeked at them through amber eyes half-covered by green shades. After they had passed, the trees whispered about it to each other.

'A real bunch of weirdos,' said a great elm.

'I think it was maybe an optical illusion,' said an oak. 'Especially that metal thing.'

'Oh, my head,' said a weeping willow. 'What a night! Let me tell you about it.'

Mishkin and the robot continued into the inner recesses of the deeper glooms where, wraith-like, the dim, indistinct memories of past arboreal splendours still clung in a pale miasma. (A kind of dying around the sacred shafts of vague luminescence that crept broken-backed down the branches of lachrymose trees.)

'It sure is gloomy in here,' Mishkin said.

'Stuff like that generally does not affect me,' the robot said. 'We robots tend to unemotionality. Empathy is built into us, however, so we come to experience everything vicariously, which is the same as experiencing it legitimately in the first place.'

'Huh,' said Mishkin.

'Because of that, I am inclined to agree with you. It is gloomy in here. It is also spooky.'

The robot was a good-hearted sort and not nearly as

mechanical as his appearance would lead one to believe. Years afterward, when he was quite red with rust and his hands had the telltale cracks of metal fatigue, he would speak to the robot youngsters about Mishkin. 'He was a quiet man,' the robot said, 'and you might have thought he was a little simpleminded. But there was a directness about him and a willingness to accept his own condition that was endearing in the extreme. Taken all in all, he was a man; we shall not see his like again.'

The robot children said, 'Sure, Grandfather,' and went away laughing behind his back. They were smooth and sharp and bright, and they thought that they were the only ones who had ever been modern, and it never occurred to them that others had been so before them and that others would be so after them. And if they had been told that someday they would be put back on the shelf with other pieces of discarded merchandise they would have laughed all the harder. That is the way of the young robots and no amount of programming seems able to change it.

But that was still in the far future. Now there was the robot and there was Mishkin, journeying together into the forest, both of them filled with knowledge of the most exquisitely detailed sort, none of it apropos to their situation. It was probably about this time that Mishkin came to his great realization – that knowledge is never pertinent to one's needs. What you need is always something else, and a wise man builds his life around this knowledge about the lack of usefulness of knowledge.

Mishkin worried around danger. He wanted to do the right thing when he faced danger. Ignorance of the appropriate action made him anxious. He was more afraid of appearing ridiculous than he was of dying.

'Look,' he said to the robot, 'we must make up our minds.

We may meet a danger at any time, and we really must decide how we will handle it.'

'Do you have any suggestions?' the robot asked.

'We could toss a coin,' Mishkin suggested.

'That,' said the robot, 'is the epitome of fatalism and quite opposed to the scientific attitude we both represent. Give ourselves up to chance after all our training? It is quite unthinkable.'

'I don't like it much, myself,' Mishkin said, 'but I think that we can agree that *no* plan of action is a disastrous course.'

The robot said, 'Perhaps we could decide each case upon its merits.'

'Will we have time for that?' Mishkin asked.

'Here's the chance to find out,' the robot said.

Up ahead, Mishkin saw something flat and thin and wide, like a sheet. It was coloured a mouse-grey. It floated about three feet above the ground. It was coming straight towards them, like everything else in Harmonia.

'What do you think we ought to do?' Mishkin asked.

'Damned if I know,' the robot said, 'I was going to ask you.'

'I don't think we could outrun it.'

'I don't think immobility would do any good,' the robot said.

'Should we shoot it?'

'Blasters don't seem to work too well on this planet. We'd probably just get it angry.'

'What if we just stroll along, minding our own business,' Mishkin said. 'Maybe it'll just leave us alone.'

'The hope of despair,' said the robot.

'Do you have any other ideas?'

'No.'

'Then let's start strolling.'

9

Mishkin and the robot were strolling through the forest one day in the merry, merry month of May when they happened to surprise a pair of bloodshot eyes in the merry, merry month of May.

Nothing is very funny when you're underneath.

'Stand up and be counted,' Mishkin's father had said to him. So Tom Mishkin stood up to be counted, and the number was one. This was not very instructive. Mishkin never stood up to be counted again.

Let's take it now from the point of view of the monster who was approaching Mishkin. Usually reliable sources tell us that the monster did not feel at all monstrous. The monster felt anxious. That is the way everyone feels except when they are drunk or high. It would be good to remember that when making any strange contacts: *The monster feels anxious.* Now, if only you can convince him that you too, despite being a monster, also feel anxious. The sharing of anxieties is the first step in communication.

'Ouch,' said Mishkin.

'What's the matter?' asked the robot.

'I stubbed my toe.'

'You'll never get out of this spot like that.'

'What should I do?'

'It might be best to continue strolling.'

The sun beat down. The forest contained many colours. Mishkin was a complicated human being with a past and a sex life and various neuroticisms. The robot was a complicated simulacrum of a man and might just as well be considered a man. The creature who was approaching them was a complete unknown but can be presumed to have had a certain pleasurable amount of complication about him. Everything was complicated.

As Mishkin approached the monster he had various fantasies, none of which are interesting enough to record.

The monster also had various fantasies.

The robot never permitted himself fantasies. He was an old-fashioned, inner-directed, Protestant ethic type of robot, and he didn't hold with tomfoolery.

There were drops of crystal clear water trembling on the green, pouting, heart-curved lips. Actually, they weren't drops of water at all; they were decals made in some loathsome factory in Yonkers. The children had decorated the trees with them.

The monster he went astrolling. He nodded civilly to Mishkin and the robot nodded civilly to the monster as they strolled past.

The monster did a double take. 'What in hell was that?' he asked.

'Beats the hell out of me,' said one of the perambulatory trees, who had moved back from the north forty in hopes of making a killing on the stock exchange.

'It seems to have worked,' Mishkin said.

'It usually does,' the robot said, 'on Darbis IV.'

'Do you suppose it would usually work here on Harmonia?'

'I don't see why not. After all, if a thing is right once, it is capable of being right an infinite number of times. The actual figure is *n* minus one, which is a very large number indeed and contains only one possibility of error out of an infinity of correct actions.'

'How often does that once come up?' Mishkin asked.

'Too damned often,' the robot told him. 'It really knocks hell out of the law of averages.'

'Well, then,' Mishkin said, 'maybe your formula is wrong.'

'Not a chance of it,' the robot said. 'The theory is right, even if it usually doesn't work out in practice.'

'I suppose that's good to know,' Mishkin said.

'Sure it is. It's always good to know things. Anyhow, we have another chance to test it out. Here comes another monster.'

10

Not everyone in the forest was capable of taking consolation from philosophy. The raemit, for example, walked along in a fog of self-loathing. The raemit knew that he was utterly and completely alone. In part this was because the raemit was the only one of his species, which tended to reinforce his feeling of isolation. But the raemit also knew that the responsibility for alienation resides with the individual and that circumstance, no matter how apparently normative, was merely the neutral ground against which the individual worked out his own internal dramas. That was a depressing thought and also a confusing one, so the raemit walked along feeling weird and spaced out and like the only raemit on Harmonia, which it was.

'What's *that*?' the raemit asked himself. He stared long and hard at the two alien creatures. Then he said, 'Hallucinations, yet. That's what having a sensitivity such as mine brings you.'

The two alien creatures or hallucinations continued walking. The raemit quickly reviewed his entire life.

'It's all a bag of shit,' the raemit concluded. 'A raemit works all his life and what happens? He gets himself into trouble with the cops, his girlfriend leaves him, his wife leaves him, and then he starts seeing hallucinations. I mean, really, *alien creatures*, what will it be next?'

11

'What I'm going to do,' said the Countess of Melba, 'I am going to take the pledge.'

'Then for the love of God Almighty,' cried the Duke of Melba, 'get on with it, *do* get on with it, and stop nattering on about it.'

'I do not believe in you any more,' the Duchess of Melba said.

At that instant the Duke of Melba vanished like the insubstantial thing he was and, as far as I'm concerned, always will be.

Mishkin remembered something that had happened to him as a little boy on a stud ranch near Abilene. But he didn't pursue it because he couldn't see how it would help him in his present circumstances, whatever they were.

'One can be on the verge of violent death,' said the robot, 'and still be bored. I wonder why that is so?'

'One can get damned sick of the thoughts of robots,' Mishkin replied.

The forest died. It was an attack of the floral version of hoof and mouth disease that had wracked such ruin around the countryside. Nothing for it, we will simply have to get along without that forest.

12

Mishkin was walking through a large parking lot. It was a beige parking lot with green and yellow stripes. The parking meters were mauve, and the crumpled old newspapers were scarlet and bronze. It was a humdinger of a parking lot.

'This seems to be a parking lot,' Mishkin remarked.

'It does seem so, doesn't it?' the Duke of Melba replied, twirling the ends of his long blond moustaches. 'Reminds me of a story. Rather good story. Friend of mine was staying at a friend's house in Surrey. Cotswolds, actually. He had retired for the night in a room that was purported to be haunted. My friend thought that a rather piquant touch, but he didn't buy it, of course. No one does. Well, then. My friend set the guttering candle down by his bedside – the place had no electricity, you see; or rather, it *did* have electricity but a sudden storm had sent it all kaput. He was just settling in for the night, in quite a calm mood, when ...'

'Excuse me,' Mishkin said. 'Who are you?'

'Duke of Melba,' said the Duke of Melba. 'But call me Clarence. I don't hold with all of that title nonsense. I don't believe I caught your name.'

'That's because I didn't throw it,' Mishkin said.

'Oh, I say, that's rather good. Original?'

'It was, once,' Mishkin said.

'Very good!'

'My name is Mishkin,' Mishkin said. 'I don't suppose you happened to see a robot anywhere around here?'

'I didn't actually.'

'Strange. He just vanished.'

'Nothing strange about that,' the Duke of Melba said. 'Just a minute ago my wife remarked that she didn't believe in me, and lo and behold, I just vanished. Strange, isn't it?'

'Very strange,' Mishkin said. 'But I suppose it does happen.'

'I suppose it does,' Clarence said. 'After all, it just happened to me. Damned funny feeling, vanishing.'

'What does it feel like?'

'Hard to put your finger on it. A sort of *insubstantial* thing, if you know what I mean.'

'You're sure you didn't see my robot?'

'Reasonably sure. I suppose you were fond of him?'

'We've been through a lot together.'

'Old war buddies,' the Duke said, nodding and untwisting his moustaches. 'Nothing quite like old war buddies. Or old wars. I remember a time outside of Ypres . . .'

'Excuse me,' Mishkin said. 'I don't know where you came from, but I think that I must warn you that you have vanished or been vanished into a place of considerable danger.'

'It's uncommonly kind of you to warn me,' the Duke said. 'But, actually, I'm in no danger at all. The danger number is your movie, whereas I am in an entirely different and much less satisfactory sequence. Projection doth make mockery of us all, as the poet said. Whimsical anachronism is more my line of country, old chap. Now, as I was saying . . .'

The Duke of Melba interrupted himself by stopping. A shadow of discontent had just crossed his mind. He was unsatisfied with his delineation of himself. All that he had presented so far was the fact that he had long blond moustaches, sounded vaguely English, and seemed a little silly. This seemed to him insufficient. He decided to rectify the situation at once.

The Duke of Melba was a large and impressive individual. His eyes were a frosty blue. He bore a resemblance to Ronald Colman, though the Duke was handsomer, more bitter, and possessed more cool. His hands were finely shaped with long tapering fingers. Noticeable also were the little crow's-feet at the corners of his eyes. These, together with the feathering of grey at his temples, did nothing to detract from his attractiveness; quite the contrary, they gave him a bold, brooding, weather-beaten appearance that the opposite sex (as well as many members of his own sex, not all of them gay) found distinctively attractive. Taken all in all, he was the man you would pick to advertise your oldest scotch, your best line of clothing, your most expensive motorcars.

The Duke thought that over and found it good. A few things were missing. So he gave himself the faintest suggestion of a limp, just for the hell of it and because he had always considered a limp to be mysterious and attractive.

When he was through, the Duke of Melba was fair pleased. The only thing that galled him was the fact that his wife had caused him to vanish. That seemed to him a very castrating thing to do.

'Do you know?' he said to Mishkin, 'I have a wife. The Duchess of Melba, you know.'

'Oh. That's nice,' Mishkin said.

'In a way it is, I suppose. But the thing is, I don't believe in her.'

The Duke smiled to himself: an attractive smile. Then he frowned: an attractive frown, for his wife appeared suddenly in front of him.

The Duchess of Melba took one good look at the Duke, then swiftly changed her appearance. Her hair went from grey to chestnut brown with red highlights. She became tall, slender, with medium-large boobies and a delicious ass. She gave herself delicate bones in her wrists, a faint, blue vein that throbbed in her forehead, a beauty mark shaped like a star on her left cheek, fantastic legs, a Pierre Cardin outfit, a Hermès handbag, shoes by Riboflavin, a tantalizing smile smiled by long, slim lips that didn't need any lipstick because they were naturally red (it ran in the family), a solid gold Dunhill lighter, emaciated cheeks, raven black hair with blue highlights, and a big sapphire ring instead of a gold-plated wedding band.

The Duke and the Duchess looked at each other and found each other admirable. They strolled away arm and arm into the nowhere they had made each other vanish into.

'All the best,' Mishkin called after them. He looked around the parking lot but he couldn't find his car. It was one of those days.

At last a parking lot attendant came ambling up to him – a short fat man in a green jumper with the words AMRITSAR HIGH SCHOOL ALL-STARS embroidered over his left breast pocket. The attendant said, 'Your ticket, sir? No tickee, no caree.'

'Here it be,' said Mishkin, and from the transverse pocket of his slung pouch he removed a piece of red pasteboard.

'Don't let him take that ticket!' a voice called out.

'Who is that?' Mishkin asked.

'I am your SPER robot presently disguised as a 1968 Rover TC 2000. You are under the influence of a hallucinating drug. Do not give the attendant that ticket!'

'Give ticket,' said the attendant.

'Not so fast,' said Mishkin.

'Yes, *fast*,' said the attendant, and reached out.

It seemed to Mishkin that the attendant's fingers split into a mouth. Mishkin stepped back. Very slowly the attendant came towards him. Now he could be seen as a kind of large snake with wings and a forked tail. Mishkin avoided him without trouble.

Mishkin was back in the forest (That damned forest!) The robot was standing beside him. A large, winged snake was advancing very slowly on Mishkin.

13

The snake had a mouth that secreted fantasies. His very breath was illusion. His eyes were hypnotic, and the movement of his wings cast spells. Even his size and shape were matters of illusion, for he was capable of changing himself from gigantic to infinitesimal. But when the snake had made himself tinier than a fly, Mishkin deftly captured him and shut him up in an aspirin bottle.

'What will you do with him?' the robot asked.

'I will keep him,' said Mishkin, 'until it is the proper time for me to live in fantasies.'

'Why is that time not now?' the robot asked.

'Because I am young now,' Mishkin replied, 'and it is time for me to be living adventures and to be making actions and suffering reactions. Later, much later, when my fires have dimmed and my memories have lost their bright edge, then I shall release this creature. The winged snake and I will walk together into that final illusion that is death. But that time is not now.'

'Well spoken,' the robot said. But he wondered who was speaking with Mishkin's mouth.

So they kept going across the forest. The aspirin bottle was sometimes very heavy, sometimes light. It was evident that the creature had power. But it was not enough to dissuade Mishkin from the work that lay ahead of him. He didn't know what this work was, but he knew that it didn't lie in an aspirin bottle.

14

Mishkin and the robot came to a ravine. There was a plank across the two sides of the ravine. Looking down, one could see a tiny thread of water thousands of feet below.

This was noteworthy, for the ravine had a natural grandeur and attractiveness. But more striking by far was the plank across the two sides of the ravine. There was a table on the plank, near the middle. There were four chairs at the table, and four men sat in the chairs. They were playing a game of cards. They had full ashtrays beside them. There was an unshielded light, suspended by nothing visible, burning palely above their heads.

Mishkin approached and listened to them for a while.

'Open for a dollar.'

'Fold.'

'Call.'

'Raise.'

'And another dollar.'

They played with concentration but with evident fatigue. Their faces were stubbly and pale, and their rolled-up sleeves were grimy. They were drinking beer from no-neck bottles and eating thick sandwiches.

Mishkin walked up and said, 'Excuse me.'

The men looked up. One of them said, 'What's up, bub?'

'I'd like to get by,' Mishkin said.

They stared at him as if he were crazy. 'So walk around,' one of the men said.

'I can't,' Mishkin said.

'Why not? You lame or something?'

'Not at all,' Mishkin said. 'But the fact is, if I tried to walk around I would fall into the ravine. You see, there's no room between the chairs and the edge; or rather, there's an inch or two, but my balance isn't good enough for me to risk it.'

The men stared at him. 'Phil, did you ever hear anything like that?'

Phil shook his head. 'I've heard some weird ones, Jack, but this takes the fur-lined pisspot for sure. Eddie, what do you think?'

'He's gotta be drunk. Huh, George?'

'Hard to say. What do you think, Burt?'

'I was just going to ask Jack what he thought,' Burt looked at Mishkin. In a not unkindly manner, he said, 'Look, fella, me and the boys are having this private poker game here in room 2212 of the Sheraton-Hilton, and you come in and say that you'll fall over the edge of a *ravine* if you walk around us, when the fact of the matter is that you shouldn't be in our room in the first place, but being here, you could walk around us all day without anything happening to you since this happens to be a hotel not a ravine.'

'I think you are labouring under a delusion,' Mishkin said. 'It happens that you are not in a hotel room in the Sheraton-Hilton.'

George, or possibly Phil, said, 'Then where are we?'

'You are seated at a table situated on a plank over a ravine on a planet called Harmonia.'

'You,' said Phil, or possibly George, 'are out of your ever-loving mind. Maybe we had a few drinks, but we do know what hotel we signed into.'

'I don't know how it happened,' Mishkin said, 'but you are not where you think you are.'

'We're on a plank over a ravine, huh?' Phil said.

'Exactly.'

'So how come we think we're in room 2212 of the Sheraton-Hilton?'

'I don't know,' Mishkin said. 'Something very strange seems to have happened.'

'Sure, it has,' Burt said. 'It's happened to your head. You're crazy.'

'If anyone is crazy,' Mishkin said, 'you people are crazy.'

The poker players laughed. George said, 'Sanity is a matter of consensus. We say it's a hotel room and we outvote you four to one. That makes you crazy.'

Phil said, 'This damned city is full of nuts. Now they come up to your hotel room and tell you it's balanced on a plank over a ravine.'

'Will you let me get by?' Mishkin asked.

'Suppose I do; where will you go?'

'To the other side of the ravine.'

'If you go around us,' Phil said, 'you'll only come to the other side of the room.'

'I don't think so,' Mishkin said. 'And, although I wish to be tolerant of your opinions, in this case I can see that they are based upon a false assumption. Let me get by and you can see for yourself.'

Phil yawned and stood up. 'I was going to the crapper, anyhow, so you can get by me. But when you reach the end of the room, will you turn around again like a good boy and get the hell out of here?'

'If it's a room, I promise to leave at once.'

Phil stood up, took two steps back from the table, and fell into the ravine. His scream echoed and re-echoed as he fell into the depths.

George said, 'Those goddamned police sirens are getting on my nerves.'

Mishkin edged past the table, holding on to its edge, and made it to the other side of the ravine. The robot followed. Once they were both safe, Mishkin called out, 'Did you see? It was a ravine.'

George said, 'While he's at it, I hope Phil gets Tom out of the crapper. He's been there about half an hour.'

'Hey,' Burt said, 'where did the nut go?'

The card players looked around. 'He's gone,' George said. 'Maybe he went into a closet.'

'Nope,' Burt said, 'I've been watching the closet.'

'Did he jump out a window?'

'You can't open the windows.'

'Too much,' George said. 'That's really one for the books . . . Hey, Phil, hurry up!'

'You can never get him out of the crapper,' Burt said. 'How about a little gin rummy?'

'You're on,' Burt said, and shuffled the cards.

Mishkin watched them for a few minutes then continued into the forest.

15

Mishkin asked the robot, 'What was that all about?'

'I am reviewing the information now,' the robot said. He was silent for a few minutes. Then he said, 'They did it with mirrors.'

'That seems unlikely.'

'All hypotheses concerning the present sequence of events are unlikely,' the robot said. 'Would you prefer me to say that we and the card players met at a discontinuity point in the space-time continuum in which two planes of reality intersected?'

'I think I would prefer that,' Mishkin said.

'Simpleminded sod. Shall we go on?'

'Let's. I just hope the car works.'

'It had better work,' the robot said. 'I spent three hours rewiring the generator.'

Their car – a white Citroën with mushroom-shaped tyres and a hydraulic tail-light system – was parked just ahead of them in a little clearing. Mishkin got in and started up. The robot stretched out on the back seat.

'What are you doing?' Mishkin asked.

'I thought I'd take a little nap.'

'Robots never sleep.'

'Sorry. I meant that I was going to take a little pseudo-nap.'

'That's OK,' Mishkin said, putting the car into gear and taking off.

16

Mishkin drove across a green and pleasant meadow for several hours. He came at last into a narrow dirt road that led between giant willow trees and then into a driveway. In front of him was a castle. He awakened the robot from his pseudo-snooze.

'Interesting,' said the robot. 'Did you notice the sign?'

In front of the castle, tacked up on a young spruce tree, was a sign reading: IMAGINARY CASTLE.

'What does it mean?' Mishkin asked.

'It means that some people have the decency to state a simple truth, and thus to avoid confusing passersby. An imaginary castle is one that has no counterpart in objective reality.'

'Let's go in and take a look at it,' Mishkin said.

'But I have just explained to you. The castle is not real. There is literally nothing to see.'

'I want to see it, anyhow,' Mishkin said.

'You have already read the sign.'

'But maybe that's a lie or a joke.'

'If you can't believe what is written plain as day,' the robot said, 'then how can you believe anything? You have observed, I hope, that the sign is exceptionally well made, and that the lettering is plain, forthright, and not at all flamboyant. In the right-hand corner is the seal of the Department of Public Works, an unimpeachable and businesslike organization whose motto is *Noli me tangere*. It is evident that they have classified this castle as a public service so that no one will walk into it thinking that he is in a real castle. Or isn't the Department of Public Works a reliable service to you?'

'It is a very acceptable reference,' Mishkin said. 'But maybe the seal is a forgery.'

'That is typically paranoid thinking,' the robot said. 'First, despite its solid and commonplace air of reality, you consider the sign a lie or a joke (the two are essentially the same thing). Then, when you learn the source of this so-called "joke", you think that perhaps it is a forgery. Suppose I succeed in proving to you the authenticity and sincerity of the sign makers? I suppose that you would insist, despite the accepted principle of Ockham's razor, that the sign makers are imaginary, or deluded, and that the castle is real.'

'It is simply a rather unusual thing,' Mishkin said, 'to come across a castle and to be told that it is imaginary.'

'I see nothing unusual about it,' the robot said. 'Since the latest revision of the truth-in-advertising statutes, ten gods, four major religions, and eighteen hundred and twelve cults to date have been labelled imaginary in accordance with the law.'

17

Guided by the sacristan – a short cheerful old man with a white beard and a wooden leg – Mishkin and the robot toured the Imaginary Castle. They went down long stuffy passageways and through short draughty cross passageways, past factory-tarnished suits of armour and pre-faded, pre-shrunk tapestries depicting virgins and unicorns in ambiguous poses. They inspected the punishment cells where make-believe prisoners pretended to suffer from the vile incursions of fraudulent racks, ersatz pincers, and fake thumbscrews wielded by stoop-shouldered torturers whose commonplace horn-rimmed glasses robbed them of any pretence to credibility. (Only the pasteurized blood was real, and not even that was convincing.) They passed the armoury where snub-nosed demoiselles typed triplicate requests for the latest model Holy Grail swords and Big Barbarian spears.

They went to the battlements and saw the vats of Smith & Wesson polyunsaturated oil suitable for low-temperature anointing or high-temperature boiling. They looked into the chapel, where a boyish, red-haired priest made jokes in Sanskrit to a congregation of Peruvian tin miners, while Judas, crucified by a contrived clerical error, looked down, bewildered, from a Symbolist cross of rare woods that had been especially selected for the spiritual sensibility of their textures.

Finally, they came to the great banquet hall, within which was a table loaded with Broasted chickens, mugs of Orange Julius, chili dogs, clams on the half shell, and two-inch slices of roast beef done crisp on the outside and rare on the inside. And there were platters of soft ice cream, and trays of pizza, both Neapolitan and Sicilian, all of them with extra cheese and sausage, anchovies, mushrooms, and capers. There were foil-wrapped heroes and poorboys, and combination, multiple-decker sandwiches of pastrami, tongue, corned beef, chopped liver, lox, cream cheese, onions, coleslaw, potato salad, and dill and half-sour pickles. And there were great tureens of kreplach soup, and chicken soup with noodles. And there were cauldrons filled with lobster Cantonese, and platters piled high with sweet and sour spareribs, and waxed-paper containers of pressed duck with walnuts. And there were roast stuffed turkeys with cranberry sauce, cheeseburgers, shrimps in black bean sauce, and much more besides.

'What happens to me if I eat some of this?' Mishkin asked.

'Nothing,' the sacristan said. 'Imaginary food cannot nourish you; but it also cannot make you sick.'

'Does it have a mental effect?' Mishkin asked, sampling a chili dog.

'It must have a mental effect,' the sacristan pointed out, 'since imaginary food is, literally, food for the mind. The precise effect varies with the intelligence and sophistication of the partaker. Among the ignorant and gullible, for example, imaginary food tends to be quite nourishing. Pseudo-nourishing, of course, but the nervous system cannot differentiate between real and imaginary events. Some idiots have managed to live for years and years on this insubstantial stuff, thus demonstrating once again the effects of belief upon the human body.'

'It tastes good,' Mishkin said, gnawing on a turkey drumstick and helping himself to a portion of cranberry sauce.

'Of course,' the sacristan said. 'Imaginary food always has the best taste.'

Mishkin ate and ate, and enjoyed himself hugely. Then, heavy-laden, he went over to a couch and lay down. The gentle insubstantiality of the couch lulled him to sleep.

The sacristan turned to the robot and said, 'Now the shit is really going to hit the fan.'

'Why?' the robot asked.

'Because, having partaken of imaginary nourishment, that young man is about to have imaginary dreams.'

'Is that bad?' the robot asked.

'It tends to get confusing.'

'Perhaps I should wake him up,' the robot said.

'Of course you should; but first, why don't we turn on the tube and tune in on his dream?'

'Can we do that?'

'You'd better believe it,' the sacristan said. He crossed the room and turned on the television set.

'That wasn't there before,' the robot said.

'One nice thing about an imaginary castle,' the sacristan pointed out, 'is that you can have pretty much what you want when and where you want it, with no necessity for tedious explanations that are always something of a bring-down.'

'Why don't you focus that screen?'

'It is in focus,' the sacristan said. 'Here come the titles.'

On the screen the following credits appeared :

Robert Sheckley Enterprises Presents
MISHKIN'S IMAGINARY DREAM
A Neo-Menippean Rodomontade
Produced in Can Pep' des Correu Studios, Ibiza

'What was that all about?' the robot asked.

'Just the usual crap,' said the sacristan. 'Here comes the dream.'

18

Mishkin was strolling along contemplating the nature of reality when a voice said to him, 'Hi.'

Mishkin started uncontrollably and looked all around. He saw no one. He was on a flat, level plain, and there was no object more than one foot high for at least five miles in any direction for anyone to hide behind.

Mishkin did not lose his cool. He answered, 'How do you do?'

'Fine, thank you. And yourself?'

'Quite well, all things considered. Have we met before?'

'I don't think so,' the voice said. 'Still, you can never tell, can you?'

'No, you can't,' Mishkin said. 'What are you doing around here?'

'I live around here.'

'It seems like a nice place.'

'It's all right,' the voice said. 'But the winters are impossibly cold and damp.'

'Really?'

'Yes. I suppose you're a tourist?'

'More or less,' Mishkin said. 'It's the first time I've been here.'

'How do you like it?'

'It's very nice. I haven't seen much yet, but what I've seen seems very nice.'

'I'm used to it all,' the voice said. 'But I suppose that's because I live here.'

'Probably,' Mishkin said. 'That's how I usually feel at home.'

'Where *is* your home, by the way?'

'Earth,' Mishkin said.

'Big red planet.'

'Small green planet.'

'I think I've heard of it. Yellowstone National Park?'

'That's the place.'

'You're a long, long way from home.'

'I suppose I am,' Mishkin said, 'But, of course, I enjoy travelling.'

'Did you come by spaceship?'

'Yes, I did.'

'I'll bet that was interesting.'

'Yes, it was.'

There was a silence. Mishkin didn't know how to bring

up the fact that he couldn't see whom he was talking to. He realized that he should have mentioned it earlier. Now he would appear foolish if he brought it up.

'Well,' the voice said, 'I suppose I'd better be getting along.'

'It's been nice talking to you,' Mishkin said.

'I've enjoyed it, too. I wonder if you've noticed that I'm invisible?'

'As a matter of fact, I have. I suppose that you can see me?'

'Yes, I can. We invisibles can see visible things such as yourself very well. Except for the unfortunate few among us who are blind, of course.'

'Can you see each other?'

'No, of course not. We wouldn't be really invisible if we could.'

'I hadn't thought of that,' Mishkin said. 'I suppose it's a bother?'

'Definitely,' the invisible said. 'We pass each other in the streets without noticing each other. That hurts people's feelings, even though they know it can't be helped. And invisibility makes falling in love difficult, too. For example, if I meet a nice young lady at the Saturday night YMCA dance I don't know if she's cute or a complete dog. And one hates to ask. I know that that sort of thing shouldn't matter, but it always seems to, doesn't it?'

'It does on Earth,' Mishkin said. 'But I suppose there are advantages to being invisible.'

'Oh, yes. We used to get a lot of pleasure out of springing out at people and saying boo. But now, everyone around here knows about us and no one is frightened anymore, they just tell us to go fuck off.'

'I suppose that being invisible is an advantage when you go hunting?'

'Not really. We invisibles tend to be pretty heavy-footed, so we make a lot of noise when we hunt, unless we stand perfectly still. Because of this we tend to hunt only a single species of animal. We call them the Unhearables, since they are all totally deaf. Against them our invisibility is a great advantage. But the Unhearables make rather mediocre eating, even potted and served with béchamel sauce.'

'I always thought that an invisible creature would have an edge over everything else,' Mishkin said.

'That's what everybody thinks,' the invisible said. 'But really, invisibility is just a kind of handicap.'

'That's too bad,' Mishkin said politely.

There was a short, uncomfortable silence.

'What do you look like?' Mishkin asked.

'Can't say, old man. Invisible, you know. Makes shaving difficult. Watch out!'

Mishkin had blundered into an invisible object and had given himself a severe rap on the forehead. He walked more slowly now, with one hand stretched out in front of him.

'How did you see that invisible object?' he asked.

'Didn't see it, old man,' the invisible told him. 'Saw the identification marker.'

Looking around him, Mishkin could see various metal plaques set into the ground. These were engraved with self-translating characters (required by interstellar law), which made them as easy to read as English is to the average literate Englishman.

Ahead of him were plaques marked, 'Rock', 'Clump of Cactus', 'Abandoned Volkswagen Microbus', 'Unconscious Person', 'Withered Fig Tree', 'Lost Dutchman Mine', and the like.

'That's very considerate,' Mishkin said, threading his way between 'Trash Heap' and 'Tourist Office'.

'It's purely selfish,' the invisible said. 'We got tired of bumping into those things ourselves.'

'How did those things become invisible?' Mishkin asked.

'Some sort of contamination. For a while everything is all right, we go about our business, get our work done. Then the objects we associate with begin to grow dim, and then they vanish entirely. For example, one fine morning a bank president finds that he can't find his own bank. No one knows if the street lights are on or off. Invisible milkmen try to deliver invisible milk in invisible bottles to the invisible occupants of invisible houses. The results are comico-pathetic. Everything gets a bit mixed up.'

'So you put out the plaques,' Mishkin said.

'No, we use the plaques only for outlying areas. Inside the city limits, we paint everything with visible paint.'

'Does that solve the problem?'

'It's a big help, but the system has certain flaws. Repainted paintings suffer an inevitable aesthetic loss. Painted people often have skin reactions. But the major flaw is that the visible paint itself tends to become invisible after varying lengths of contact with invisible objects. We try to handle this by a continual repainting programme based upon statistical, positional, and temporal charts of all objects in the city. But even given the efficiency of our programme, many things still get lost. There are incalculable variables, you see: despite stringent quality controls, no two batches of visible paint are completely identical in their characteristics. Each batch is affected uniquely by the different combinations, intensities, and durations of temperature-humidity interactions. The changing planetary and lunar relationships may also be a factor. And there are other factors still under investigation.'

The invisible sighed. 'We try not to give way to despair. Our scientists work continually on the project of making ourselves permanently visible. Some call it a visionary and unrealistic hope; but we know that others, such as yourself, have achieved the bliss of visibility. So why not us?'

'I never thought it would be like this,' Mishkin said. 'I had always thought that it would be fun to be invisible.'

'Don't you believe it,' the invisible said. 'Invisibility is just about the same as being blind.'

19

Desert gave way to semi-desert. Mishkin and the robot walked through a flat, arid wasteland, past lost dirt roads, stunted shrubs, and an occasional deserted frame house.

They crossed a little rise and saw a man in a tuxedo with a tall black hat on his head sitting on a black metal suitcase. In front of him were rusty railroad tracks that stretched for fifty feet on either side.

'Christ,' the robot said, 'another creep.'

'Don't be rude,' Mishkin told him. He walked up and greeted the stranger.

'About time someone came along,' the stranger said. 'I've been sitting here for two days, and I don't mind telling you it's getting pretty boring.'

'What are you waiting for?' Mishkin asked.

'The 12:10 from Yuma,' the stranger said, turning to the left and looking down the fifty feet of track. 'But they don't run the trains on time any more.'

'I don't think this particular train runs at all any more,' Mishkin said.

'I wouldn't be surprised,' the stranger said. 'It does seem unlikely, taking everything into consideration. But I sure as hell can't walk any more. And maybe something'll happen and the train *will* come by. I've seen stranger things happen. Strange things do happen for me. I suppose you know who I am.'

'I'm afraid that I don't,' Mishkin said.

'You must be pretty ignorant because I'm pretty famous. In this manifestation I am Ronsard the Magnificent, and I am probably the greatest magician the universe has ever seen.'

'Lotta crap,' the robot mumbled.

'Don't let appearances deceive you,' Ronsard said. 'There is a reason why I am currently playing whistle-stops and waiting for nonexistent trains in freaky places. Karma catches up with us all, eh? But something always turns up. Would you like to witness some magic?'

'I would like that very much,' Mishkin said.

'It's a lotta bullshit,' the robot said.

Ronsard ignored the sullen mechanical. 'For my first number I will do the rabbit trick.'

'I've seen it,' the robot said.

'I haven't,' Mishkin said. 'So kindly shut up.'

The robot leaned back and crossed his arms. A mean, sceptical smile was upon his metallic face, and the very angles of his body spelled disbelief. Mishkin leaned forward eagerly, his hands clasped around his knees. The very attitude of his body spelled willingness to be astonished.

Ronsard opened up his suitcase and took out a complicated control board, two automobile batteries, a jumble of wires, three circuit boards, a flask filled with a murky-looking fluid, and a small accelerometer. He hooked up wires between these objects and connected them to a red and black lead that he attached to the brim of his hat. He took out a circuit tester and tested. Then he turned to Mishkin.

'You will observe, my dear sir, that the hat is empty.' He showed his hat to Mishkin and the robot, who yawned.

'Now, then,' the magician said. He took a white satin cloth from his suitcase and laid it over the hat. Then he made passes with his right hand and said, 'Rje-Sgampo Rinpoche-hi Lam Mchog Rinpoche Hi Hrheng-wa Zhes Bya-wa Bzhugs-so.' At last he kicked the control board with his right heel.

There was a crackle of sparks and a loud hissing sound. Gauges spun then returned to normal.

The magician removed the cloth. From the hat he pulled a live rabbit. He put it down on the ground and bowed.

Mishkin applauded. 'He does it with mirrors,' sneered the robot.

The rabbit tried to climb back into the hat. The magician pushed it away.

'All magicians pull rabbits out of hats,' the robot said.

'It's part of the warm-up,' said the magician.

'There's nothing supernatural about what I do,' said the magician. 'I deal in illusions, which are appearances created by careful preparation, skill, and the right equipment. That's all there is to it.'

'What exactly is an illusion?' Mishkin asked.

'Everything phenomenal can be considered an illusion,' the magician said. 'Next, I am going to do a card trick. Don't groan, sir. [This was directed to the robot.] I know that it doesn't seem like much. But my stage effects are carefully planned as to intensity and cumulative effect. Card tricks are amusing, though not fantastical or astonishing, and they allow a heightening of receptivity before the major events of the evening (the afternoon, actually). Accordingly . . .'

The magician took a deck of cards from his suitcase.

'Here we have a deck of ordinary playing cards. I will now pass these cards among you. You may examine them to your heart's content. You will find them factory sealed, unmarked in any way.'

He gave the deck to Mishkin, who broke open the package and looked them over. The robot also examined them. While they were doing this, the magician had opened his suitcase again and had taken from it three parabolic mirrors on tripods, a battery-operated computer complete with batteries, and a small radarscope. He set up the mirrors to face in various directions, and connected them to the radarscope and the computer. He took the cards and fanned them in front of one of the mirrors. He punched information into the computer. Then he waited until the radarscope gave off a high-pitched beep.

The magician took a rickety wooden folding table from the suitcase and set it up in front of them. He put the deck of cards face down on the table.

'Note that I do not at any time retain any physical hold on the cards, so I cannot be accused of forcing a choice on you. Now I would like you to shuffle the cards thoroughly and select one. Do not let me see the card you select. Remember the card.'

Mishkin and the robot did as they were told. Mishkin shuffled three times, and the robot shuffled twenty-seven times, randomizing the cards past any possibility of inherent or adherent patterns. Then they picked a card.

'Look at the card carefully, fix it in your memories. Now return the card to the deck and shuffle again.'

Again Mishkin shuffled three times and the robot shuffled twenty-seven times. (The robot would have made an excellent Canasta shuffler and had in fact been offered that lucrative position at the North Miami Beach Community Centre.)

'Now,' the magician said, 'take the number of your card – counting eleven for all court cards – and multiply by seventeen. If the resultant is even, add seven, if odd, subtract two. Determine the square root of the new number to three places. Take the last digit, add nine, and factor it according to suit – black suits are imaginary numbers, red suits are real numbers. Add to this any real number you please between one and ninety-nine. Have you followed all that?'

'Easily,' said the robot.

'What is the number?'

'Eighty-seven.'

The magician fed information into the computer, which began to spew paper. The magician studied the readout.

'Your card is the Jack of Diamonds.'

'Correct,' said the robot, and Mishkin hastily nodded.

'Still . . . Everybody does card tricks,' the robot said.

'I never claimed not to be everybody,' the magician said.

'I suppose he'll saw a woman in half next,' the robot whispered to Mishkin.

'For my next illusion,' the magician said, 'I will saw a woman in half.'

'This ought to be something,' Mishkin said.

'He does it with mirrors,' the robot said.

Years afterward, Mishkin remembered the magician's face: a long American face, putty and rose over hard white bone. His blue eyes were mirrors of the unredeemed landscape; and when the mirrors became windows, they showed an interior landscape identical to the exterior. It was a face turned hopefully towards dreams but shaped irrevocably by nightmares. The face was finally more memorable than the deeds that its owner performed.

The magician reached into his suitcase and took out a

black-haired woman with violet eyes, wearing a Piaget dress and carrying a Vuitton handbag. She winked at Mishkin and said, 'I'll try anything once.'

'She always says that,' the magician said. 'She doesn't realize that to try something once is to try it always.'

Years later the young woman said to a girlfriend, 'I was kinda freaky in those days. Man, I even let myself be sawed in half by a crazy magician. What do you think about that?'

The magician took a high-speed portable rotary saw from his suitcase, tried to start it, couldn't. He took an electric outlet from his suitcase, plugged in the saw, and started it.

'Was it one of those fakey sideshow numbers?' the friend asked.

'Like hell, fake! This magician creep, the Great Dermos or Thermos, or something, was strictly on a reality trip. He was about as fake as the Mayo Brothers. He never even *thought* of faking anything. That's why I dug him. But he was also a creep.'

From his suitcase the magician removed a four-man team of surgeons and one anaesthesiologist, all of them scrubbed, gowned, and masked. He then took out trays of surgical instruments, bottles of anaesthetics, and an operating table complete with overhead lights and drains.

The dark-haired young lady stretched out on the operating table. She was very lovely and brave. A moment like that was worth being sawed in half for.

The magician turned on the saw and approached the young lady.

At that moment a man stepped out of the suitcase. He was

fiftyish, balding, fat, in no way prepossessing except for his sudden appearance. In a loud, trembling voice he said, 'I speak out against this marriage in the name of humanity and common sense!'

'Not yet!' the magician hissed.

The man apologized and crept back into the suitcase.

Orpheus with his lyre made songs; Ronsard with his saw made cuts. Slowly (sadistically?) he lowered the whirling saw until it was poised just above the bare, brave midriff of the girl who would try anything once. The girl said, 'Man, I've really gotten myself into it this time.' The anaesthesiologist injected Num-Zit into her stomach. The surgeons made squeaky sounds with their rubber gloves.

Cut! The magician lowered his saw and made a tentative cut across the transverse brisket, gritted his teeth audibly and went to work.

The saw bit deep. Blood spurted like water from a garden hose gone berserk. Gouts of gore were thrown into the air in steep parabolas of terror. The surgeons moved in quickly, repairing the rent flesh with bought clamps and sponges and sutures.

'It's a pretty good stunt,' said the robot.

'I don't think I like it,' Mishkin said.

The saw cut through major veins and arteries. The surgeons, working with the precision of a really good ballet troop, stitched and patched. The lady said, 'Ouch,' and the anaesthesiologist administered another five ccs of Num-Zit, and a dollop of Payne-Eeze for good measure.

The stomach was cut through and patched with Scotch Brand Body Tape.

'Have I time to fuse this disc?' one of the surgeons asked.

'Stick to essentials,' said Dr Zorba.

The spine was cut through and repaired with two plastic

shirt stays and half a pint of Elmer's Glue. The magician continued sawing right through the table. The anaesthesiologist pulled a carpenter from the trunk, who repaired the damage on the spot. The young lady smiled bravely. The magician turned off his saw and bowed to Mishkin and the robot.

'For my next illusion,' the magician said, 'in front of your very eyes, I will . . .'

He stopped. They all heard the wail of a train whistle. Soon the train itself appeared, steam-operated, three cars long, laying track as it went.

'Sorry I can't complete the act,' the magician said, stepping aboard the first car. 'But that's how it goes. Something always turns up.'

'Ticket,' said the conductor.

The magician produced a ticket from his hat. Slowly, the train got under way. Ronsard called out, 'How did you like the act?'

'It was great!' Mishkin said.

'That was nothing,' said the magician. 'Wait until you see the finale.'

'When will that be?'

'It is happening now!'

'What's happening?' Mishkin called. 'Who are you?'

But the train was too far away for him to hear Ronsard's reply if, indeed, he made any.

Mishkin and the robot watched until the train was out of sight. Then Mishkin said, 'I've got a funny feeling about all this.'

'Mirrors,' the robot sneered. 'Big talk and cheap stage effects.'

They stood under a sky that reflected the earth that reflected the sky and discussed mirrors and stage effects.

20 Robot Follies

The robot had not always been of a suchness. Once he had known the splendour of youth. He, too, had drifted beneath laurel, under a willow-eyed sky. He, too, had wept at shadows, fought love, and conquered feeling. A child of Hephaestus, of the earth truly, he was the unwilling respondent of those programmatic outlooks which find identity only in similarity.

A robot may be defined as the sum of his relationships plus eighty-eight pounds of metal and plastics.

Robots desire soft things, the better to appreciate their own hardness. Robots of the Schenectady area worship a being they call White Leather Man. No Freud of the robots has come forth to explain this output.

When robots come they spurt hot grease, just like automobiles.

Robots mimic eating. There is a black robot who lives on 125th Street and drives a pink Cadillac. There are Jewish robots skilled in exegesis, whose parts drip chicken fat. There are homosexual robots who dance and lust.

Once upon a time a young robot wandered far from his factory. Lost and alone, he moved through a deep forest . . .

How well our robot remembered! A sort of madness came over him. Opacity of desire seemed a response that one could live by. He saw Mishkin as imperfect yet lovable. This was programming; he knew he did not know how to escape it.

21 Ancestral Voices Prophesying Predictability Experimental Psychoses Produced by Experimental Psychotics

'Mishkin! Come in here! You have nothing to lose but your preconceptions!'

'Price of admission – your premise.'

'Come, Mishkin lad, forget that dreary old business of the missing part. Let go of it and live a life at this moment.'

'Hang up your logic over there.'

'The only way out of the systems of repetition-compulsion is through novelty. Singularity instead of regularity. You must never predict your response. You must go through the world as if it were the world.'

'Mishkin! You must not live as though your life were a preparation for living. Preparation is an illusion. What you thought you were preparing for is what you are doing right now, which is preparing.'

'Prince Mishkin, I beg you to wake up and realize who you are.'

'You search for an object fixed in your memory like a rock in a shallow pond. Touching, perhaps, but not convincing. Do you think that you still must search? Right now, you may be solving future searches without even knowing it!'

'Here, Mishkin, is the egg you will be looking for!'

'I lost my beloved's shoe under distressing circumstances. But now Mishkin has found it.'

'It's right over here, Mishkin – the Holy Grail!'

'Upon my word! He's found the lost city of Atlantis!'

'Shiver me timbers! He's discovered the Lost Dutchman mine!'

'Be damned if he hasn't stumbled across the Holy Sepulchre!'

'This attack upon your purpose is deadly dangerous, but not to be simplemindedly resisted. Some things that devour us enhance us. Sometimes we must stand still and let ourselves be eaten.'

'Open the gates! Let Mishkin pass through!'

'I smell memory leakage. Someone around here is not paying attention.'

'Mishkin has found the White Goddess!'

'And also the pot of gold at the end of the rainbow; the secret cave where the sirens dwell; the tomb of Charlemagne; the Hall of Barbarossa; the Sibylline Books; the Philosopher's Stone – to name but a few.'

Mishkin lived in a nice little house with a nice little wife, a nice little grape arbour. Almost everything he had was nice and little. There were exceptions, of course: specifically, a nice big dog, and a not nice big chair, and a not nice little car. Still, almost everything else was as nice as you could get it and as little as you could hope for.

One day

FUTUREFLASH!

At first glance he seemed an old man: his white hair, palsied walk, dribbly lower lip, faded eye, and blotched hand all argued that he was on the wrong side of seventy. What a surprise, then, to discover that his actual chronological age was a mere twenty-three.

'A single event did harrow me thus,' quavered the oldster.

'It must have been exceptionally heavy,' Mishkin remarked.

'It will be,' the old man said. 'You see, due to a faulty relay in the space-time continuum, I remembered an event that I will only experience in the future. The verb tenses get a little tricky, but I'm sure you know what I mean.'

'I think so,' Mishkin said. 'But what is or was or will be this experience that you will have and that has already altered you so drastically?'

'Young man,' said the old man, 'I was there when Earth fought its last and greatest fight against the Black Hell Creatures from Far Arcturus.'

'Tell me about it,' Mishkin said.

'I was just about to,' the old man said and made himself as comfortable as he could, considering the brittleness of his bones.

23 Earth versus the Black Hell Creatures from Far Arcturus

Captain John McRoy's Superdreadnaught-class XK-12X spaceship, on picket duty out beyond the Southern Ridge Belt Stars, was the first to pick up the signal that all Terra was soon to know and to dread. But this was at the beginning, and the first hint of anything wrong came when Radioman 2nd Class Rip Halliday came to the captain's cabin with a worried look on his homely, freckled face.

'Take a pew, Rip,' the captain boomed. 'Drink? Lee Pan Hao, our friendly Cantonese cook, has brewed up some high-energy cocoa that really does the trick. Or how about some tollhouse cookies made with real Martian chocolate?'

'No, thanks, Captain, nothing right now.'

'Then slouch back in that easy chair and let's hear what's on your mind.'

Rip Halliday slouched back but with a hint of respectful attentiveness. In that age, when a perfect classlessness was observed by all superiors, the utmost informality prevailed. The system worked because inferiors never presumed above their station and always maintained a perfect measure of respect.

'Well, sir, I was . . .'

'Please, Rip, no "sirs" in this cabin. Just call me John.'

'Well, sir, John, I was doing a routine sweep of the 6B2 radio bands, but this time I was using a zero-beat random selector just to see how it worked. If you remember the Thalberg-Martin equations, sir, they postulate . . .'

The captain grinned and held up a broad, muscular pink hand. 'Radio's *your* field, Rip. I'm just an intergalactic truck driver. I've never gotten beyond the sigma series transformations. So put it into plain English – what did you pick up?'

'A signal,' Rip answered promptly. 'It came across loud enough to dent my ear before the AFC cut in.'

The captain nodded. 'No cause for alarm, is there? I suppose it was a radio star effect?'

Halliday shook his head. 'None in the vicinity.'

'Deflection reading?'

'Not possible, given our present speed and coordinates.'

'No chance it was a mechanically produced static effect – maybe caused by a concentration of cosmic debris grinding together?'

'No chance, sir. The configuration pattern is completely different. And what's more, the signal I got was *frequency-modulated.*'

The captain whistled softly. 'No natural discharge could account for that!'

'No, sir, John. Intelligent life produced those patterns.'

'Um,' said the captain.

'Any chance it might be a ship of ours broadcasting?' Rip asked hopefully.

The captain shook his head. 'The nearest Terran patrol ship is clear on the other side of Fiona II.'

Rip whistled softly. 'I was afraid of that!'

The captain nodded. 'It means that we've just contacted alien intelligent life of a type completely unknown to us, and we're closing with them fast.

'This is Earth's first contact with alien intelligent life,' the captain said softly to Rip. 'I think you'd better tell Marv Painter that we need a translation of those alien impulses, pronto.'

Rip Halliday's freckles stood out darker against the sudden pallor of his face. 'I'm on my way, John. Sir, I mean.'

The door dilated to allow the red-haired radioman to pass. Alone, the captain sat and stared at the stereographs of his wife and three sons. He drank a glass of Gatorade in complete silence. Then he pushed the intercom button.

He told the crew that, unless proven otherwise, they would proceed upon the assumption that they had contacted alien life of unknown intentions. But he did not tell them about the Rand-Orey equations that predicted an unfriendly first contact at 98.7 per cent probable. His orders were not to disclose this until intention had been indicated clearly. Anticipation of disaster would have impaired the efficiency of the smoothly functioning machine that was the crew.

Engineer Duff McDermott paced stumpily along the lower catwalk, then stopped to inspect the drive gauges for the twentieth time in an hour. The needles hung placidly in the green, as McDermott knew they would. But he couldn't stop himself from looking at them since he knew that contact moment was only 2.0045 hours away.

'Waddya think they'll look like?' asked Andy Tompkins, second assistant engineer's mate, his prominent adam's apple bouncing below his good-humoured, absentminded face.

'Like something out of hell,' McDermott replied. He was to remember that answer later and to wonder if there wasn't something to the discredited notion of stress-induced prescience.

'Marv,' the captain asked, 'how is it going?'

'Pretty good,' said Marv Painter, the shy, skinny, red-haired cybernetic genius. 'We should have an intelligible readout as soon as I splice in this zero-null regenerative impulse rejector into the image repro circuit and cross-tie the translator bank into the computer's second-stage input bank.'

'You mean we'll be able to understand them?' Captain McRoy asked.

'Shucks, yes. It won't be an exact translation because we don't have a vocab match up. But if we set the computer to sound-match in terms of probabilities of meaning and maintain a constant feedback loop to further refine hierarchic distinctions then we ought to get an accurate analogic reading. But that's just my own haywire idea on it, sir. If you would care to try another approach . . .'

'Marv,' said McRoy, 'the primary law of interplanetary cooperation is, let those who can, do, and let those who can't sit in the parlour with their fingers up their noses and their mouths shut and drink their coffee. I'm just a spaceship driver and you're the cyberneticist around here, and what you say goes as long as you're speaking in terms of your admittedly limited speciality.'

'Thanks for the vote of confidence, Cap,' said Marv, flashing a smile. 'If they worked governments on Earth like you run a ship it'd be clear sailing for the human race.'

'None of that, now,' the captain said with gruff, old-fashioned modesty. 'I just follow the rules, use plain common sense, temper justice with mercy, and treat every person as an entire world-system and end unto himself despite social differences imposed by a functional ranking system. Is that rig of yours working yet?'

Marv Painter turned on the set. The video repeater came to life, revealing the interior of an alien spaceship. Within, a creature sat at the controls. He was bipedal; but any resemblance to humanity began and ended there. The creature was jet green, about eight feet tall, and massively constructed. He appeared to have a chitinous exoskeleton. Antennae grew from his forehead, and his eyes extended on stalks. He had a large loose mouth behind which could be seen double rows of pointed white teeth, as on a shark.

The alien spoke: 'Much greetings, inferior, wormlike, barely sentient life forms. I am Thanatos Superbum, Captain-General of the Malachite Brood, Lord of the Vulture Redoubt, Duke Extraordinary to the O'Neills, and various other titles both hereditary and conferred. Down upon your knees, baseborn scum, and make nice to your mental, moral, and physical superior. Give your name, rank, and serial number and explain in twenty words or less why I should not grind your puny bones into pulp. Over.'

'He talks funny,' said Engineer McDermott.

'Funny and mean,' said the captain, frowning purposively. 'And also weird.'

'A lot of that,' said Marv, 'is because the computer has to analogize the alien's speech into the nearest Terran idioms, selecting from expressions it has at its disposal in its memory banks. So, of course, it comes out sounding kinda weird.'

'But are the emotional and informational connotations approximately correct?' the captain asked.

'I'm afraid so,' Marv said unhappily.

'Then it looks like we got a problem on our hands. My first impression is that this alien is unfriendly.'

'That's my impression, too,' Marv said unhappily. 'Sir, I think he's waiting for an answer.'

'I'll give him one,' the captain said, and turned on the microphone. Angry words boiled up in his mind like gas expanding according to Boyle's Law. But he forced himself to activate the Martins-Turner Interpersonal Equations, which were part of the hypno-training of every human beyond Intelligence Level IV. Instantly, the captain was icy calm and capable of objective judgment. He thought, *'I have heard words which may or may not represent an objective reality. In any event I will not respond emotionally but will try (a) to deal objectively with the situation and (b) to manipulate it (if possible) to the needs of Earth and mankind.'*

Thank God for Korzybski! the captain thought. He said into the microphone, 'Greetings, Thanatos Superbum. I am in command of this ship. My name is McRoy. I am friendly and peaceable, as are all of my race. I want to make nice with you, and I sincerely hope that you want to make nice with me.'

'Blood, sweat, and sneers!' exclaimed Superbum. 'I smell the blood of an Americun! To hell with making nice – not peace but a sword! Let one claw scratch the other. L'audace, toujours l'audace. If at first they don't succumb, trumb, trumb agun.'

'Even allowing for anachronism-generating analogies,' the captain said, 'this fellow sounds mean, hysterical, and full of trouble.' The captain turned on the microphone and asked Superbum if things couldn't be settled peacefully.

'Peace is for Commie fags,' sneered the alien. 'But I will make an offer. You may choose to be annihilated at once by the inconceivable force of our deadly ray guns, after which our space fleet will destroy your space fleet, after which we will conquer Earth and implant special radio circuits in the brains of all humans thus rendering them our slaves and subject to various fates worse than death; or you can choose the other alternative.'

'Which is?'

'Just about the same thing, only we will be nicer about it if you don't resist.'

'Both choices are unacceptable,' Captain McRoy said grimly.

'Then I can only say, watch yourself, break clean in the clinches, and may the best sentient creature win, and guard yourself at all times, stranger, 'cause me and the boys aim to purely kick the shit out of yore bunch and we ain't pertekeler about how we go about it.'

The captain signed off and grimly ordered his men to action stations. He mentally adjusted his skin temperature and adrenalin rate, for he had a feeling that this was going to be a time of hard testing.

24 Another Level Heard From

In a place whose location cannot be expressed in space-time equivalencies three beings met. For the purpose of the meeting, they had taken on terraform appearance, though this was not 'normal' for any of them. The leader, acknowledged by ethical development, called himself Ka for purposes of reference. A faint nimbus glowed around his heroic body and magnificently sculptured head.

'There is no need to explain anything,' Ka said. 'All of us gathered here know that the spacefleets of Earth and Superbum have been destined to clash according to the immutable laws of dualism. We also know that Earth represents a lot of good things that we approve of, whereas Superbum is an incarnate process of evil and a really bad thing. I think that it is superfluous to mention that it is vital for our own interests that Earth wins this battle. We are also aware that, as matters stand at present and without our intervention, Earth stands very little chance indeed. Are we all agreed that we need not discuss these matters?'

The other two beings signified their assent. One of them, De-Ao, said, 'I also agree that we need not discuss what is obvious to us. Therefore, the only question that remains is what form our intervention should take and at what moment it should occur.'

The third being, Maening, said, 'My analysis agrees with the previously stated analyses. There remains only the question of what we should do, and when, which I need not state since it has been both inferred and stated.'

'I am afraid,' said Ka, 'that we must not permit ourselves to assist Earth in any way.'

The two looked at him in consternation.

'Earth must stand on its own,' said Ka, 'for reasons which

become apparent to you if you take a moment to do some tenth level Fournean rationalizing.'

The others did so and came up with an answer identical to Ka's.

'It is a heavy result,' said Maening.

25 The Emergency Supply Service

'We supply what you need when you need it,' Mr Monitor said.

'That is exactly the kind of service I need,' said Mishkin.

'Of course you do. Everybody does. In today's world of increasing complications it's really too much to expect people to solve their own problems. They wouldn't have time left to do anything else. People should do their thing. Our thing is supplying what is needed to solve other people's problems. Your thing is presumably something else. We do our thing and you are able to do your thing. That leaves everybody happy.'

'It sounds too good to be true,' Mishkin said.

'It is,' Mr Monitor said.

'The thing I need,' Mishkin said, 'is a spare engine part, number L-1223A.'

'To hear is to obey. Are you prepared to pay for this thing?'

'Charge it to my account.'

'You are a customer after my own heart. One spare engine part number L-1223A, coming up.'

Mr Monitor showed Mishkin his write-ups in *The New York Times*, *New York Magazine*, and the *Village Voice*. All of them were raves. What better recommendations could anyone ask? Mr Monitor departed.

Mishkin sat down on a stump and waited. After a few hours he heard the noise of a motorcycle. He saw a man in a fringed leather jacket and a chamois beanie come riding through the forest. Strapped to the back of the motorcycle was a large parcel.

Fifty yards from Mishkin the motorcyclist ran across a land mine. The man, the cycle, and the package were blown to bits.

'Easy come, easy go,' Mishkin said.

26

Mishkin was clowning along through the forest, digging the sights and smells and sounds, feeling the air, really making it big in a spiritual way. He had a song without words on his lips, and his fingers snapped in time to inconceivable rhythms. It was in this mood that he came across a man leaning against a tree.

The man's eyes were closed. He didn't seem to be breathing, but he didn't seem to be dead, either. His chest was bare and there was a small bronze plaque on it. The plaque read, TURN ME ON. Above it was a toggle switch.

Mishkin turned the switch.

The man's eyes opened immediately. He clutched his forehead and swayed out of control and would have fallen if Mishkin had not caught him and lowered him gently to the ground.

'Thank you, dear sir,' the man said. 'My name is perhaps Alex Gonkin and I am much obliged to you; though perhaps it would have been better if you had left me turned off, for now, with my consciousness returned, my fear threatens to overthrow the precarious sanity of my mind.'

'What seems to be the trouble?' Mishkin asked.

'I heard the voice that said, "In order to kill him, we must kill all of his hims." I saw at once that the secret of survival was to conceal the fact that one's self was many. This could be called the first line of defence. The second line of defence was the presence of the selves and their intercommunication. I knew at once that my selves had to be killed simultaneously, or as near to simultaneity as possible, to prevent my selves from learning what was happening and taking appropriate defensive action. Do you follow me?'

'I think so,' Mishkin said.

'Then you're crazy, and I stand mute. Now we will have a few words from my Accusator.'

The Accusator lowered himself from a tree and stood before Mishkin reproachfully munching an apple.

'Thou shalt not turn on what has been turned off,' said the Accusator.

'Listen,' Mishkin said, 'if God hadn't meant this man to be turned on He wouldn't have put a toggle switch on his chest.'

'True ... But in His ineffable wisdom God caused the toggle switch to be capable of being turned off.'

'But God also put a plaque on his chest which read TURN ME ON.'

'Exegesis is a dangerous conceit,' said the Accusator.

'I didn't mean to indulge in it,' Mishkin said. 'But the moral is clear enough to me : namely that people with toggle switches in their chests shouldn't dump on you.'

'What was that?' the Accusator shouted. 'What did you say? Are you absolutely out of your mind?'

'What did I say?' Mishkin asked. 'What happened? Where am I?'

'Your actions will be studied,' said the Accusator, 'and we will let you know the results of our deliberations.'

27 In the Hall of Distorting Mirrors

Automatism can be induced in people. Indeed, you might say that automatism *is* people. We are under the control of our emotions. We float here and there on currents of what we want and what we don't want, what we desire and what desires us.

Still, take an object, any object. An orange. But the mind rejects an orange, it is round and orange – paradoxically square. Let's take something else. But now we are stuck with the orange. Thick, pockmarked skin. Any number of associations to orange, most of them banal. Orange must be struck from the list of permissible objects to associate to.

No more truck with oranges, and no more trucking of oranges. Oranges occupy entirely too prominent a place. Take an orange. We've taken enough oranges. The orange is a placebo of the mind. Why not take an intestine? Easily visualized, capable of producing many novel trips. But intestines are tediously labyrinthine. Intestines go round and round and come out orange. Intestines are filled with unpleasant matter. Perhaps it's best to go back to oranges.

Take an orange. Take it quickly before it takes you. The world of the orange is perhaps not entirely incomprehensible.

Take the subject of Mishkin and oranges. For many years Mishkin had not thought much of oranges. *Apparently*. But in truth we know that a thing's absence implies its presence. Thus, we infer the presence of oranges in Mishkin's mind, and from that we can begin to deduce many other relationships.

One thing is certain: Mishkin never knew consciously about his negative infatuation with oranges. Mishkin and the anti-orange. Oranges and the anti-Mishkin.

We must not, however, make the error of positing simple opposition. Mishkin's overdetermined disregard for oranges might not imply an opposite. More likely the figure of speech we are looking for is the oxymoron: the mating of opposites. Incongruities are not reciprocal. Reciprocity is lost in the oxymoron.

28

'The beast that kills by boredom,' said the robot, 'is also found in these parts. His voice is firm and authoritative. His statements are unchallengeable and unbelievable. His appearance is unimpeachable and obnoxious. You meet him and wish him dead, although he had done nothing wrong, absolutely nothing. He speaks to you about this in a reasonable manner. The tension becomes unbearable. Your inability to act induces apathy, which is heightened by the extreme monotony of your situation. Since you cannot kill him, you kill yourself.'

'Where is he now?' Mishkin asked.

'Boring fish for his dinner. He does this by lecturing to them on their inalienable rights.'

'I beg your pardon,' a fish said. 'No fish has ever been bored to death.'

'Go get stuffed,' the robot snarled.

29 Confusion Termed Key to Understanding

Upon a flat white rock Mishkin saw a white princess telephone. As he came up to it the telephone began ringing.

Mishkin picked it up and said, 'Hello.'

'Tom? Tom Mishkin? Is that you?'

'It is,' Mishkin said. 'Who is this?'

'This is your uncle, Arnold Epstein. Tom, how is everything?'

'Not bad,' Mishkin said. 'I've got a few problems ...'

'Who hasn't? But your health, is it good?'

'Fine, Uncle Arnold. And yours?'

'Not bad, considering. Tom, it's good to hear your voice.'

'Uncle Arnold, how did you happen to call me here?'

'It was a free gift from the A & P. I was the millionth customer for the morning and they awarded me a basket of groceries and one telephone call to anyone I wanted to call anywhere.'

'Well, it's nice that you called me, I appreciate it.'

'It's been a pleasure for me to hear your voice. Listen, Tom, your parents, are they well?'

'Fine,' Mishkin said.

'And your sister?'

'She's fine. She's in Europe.'

'That's nice. And where are you, I didn't quite understand the operator.'

'I'm on a planet called Harmonia.'

'Is it a nice place?'

'I suppose so.'

'Well, have a nice vacation. Tom, is there anything I can do for you?'

'As a matter of fact, there is,' Mishkin said. 'Have you got a pencil and a piece of paper?'

'You know me, Tom, I'm never without them.'

'Then write down Engine Part L-1223A. I need it very badly.'

'I got it written down. Don't they have a Sears, Roebuck where you are?'

'No, Uncle Arnold, they haven't got anything like that. Harmonia is a sort of undeveloped place.'

'Like Tobago?'

'Even worse. Uncle Arnold, I need that engine part right now, by the fastest shipping service available.'

'Tom, it's as good as done. You remember Seymour Gulstein, the son of your Aunt Rachel's best friend, Gertie? Well, Seymour is a field expeditor for F. B. Crowley Interplanetary Delivery Systems. I'll get the engine part this afternoon and put it in his hands and he'll get it to you in a couple of hours, a day at the most.'

'That's great, Uncle Arnold. Will it really be that fast?'

'You can count on it, Tom. When has your Uncle Arnold ever failed you?'

'I don't know how to thank you, Uncle Arnold.'

'Think nothing of it, Tom. Stay well. Give me a call when you get home.'

Mishkin hung up, leaned back, and relaxed. If his Uncle Arnold said it would be done it would be done. Governments might promise more than they could deliver, scientists might be overoptimistic about what they could accomplish, robots might have exaggerated ideas of their power; but Uncle Arnold actually made the world run while everyone else stood around trying to get it together. Uncle Arnold was maybe a little dull but absolutely irreplaceable. The turtle upon whose back Hercules stood when he held the Earth on his shoulders – that turtle was also called Arnold.

30

Mishkin and the robot came to a tree. At the end of its branches there were blue eyes with thick eyebrows. All of the eyes swivelled to stare at Mishkin.

'I *thought* you would come by this way,' the tree said, speaking from a speaker in its trunk. 'I hope that you will not deny that you are Thomas Mishkin?'

'That's who I am,' Mishkin said. 'Who are you?'

'I am a bill collector disguised as a tree,' said the bill collector disguised as a tree.

'For Chrissakes,' Mishkin said. 'Did you follow me all the way to Harmonia?'

'Indeed, I did. It's rather a curious story. Mr Oppenheimer, head of the Ne Plus Ultra Collection Agency for which I work, got an inspiration while stoned on acid at his local Tai Chi Chuan class. It suddenly occurred to Oppenheimer that the essence of life lies in completions, and a man can only judge his life in reference to the thoroughness with which he has played his life role. Hitherto, Oppenheimer had been an easygoing fellow who followed the usual practice of collecting the easily collectable debts and making a few ominous noises on the difficult ones, but ultimately saying to hell with them. Then Oppenheimer achieved his satori. To hell with mediocrity, he decided, if I'm head of a bill-collecting agency, then I'm going to make an ethic and a goal out of bill collecting. The world may very well never understand me; but perhaps future generations will be able to judge the terrible purity of my motives.

'And so Oppenheimer embarked upon the poignant and quixotic course that will probably bankrupt him within a year. He called all of us collectors into the Ready Room. "Gentlemen," he said, "this time we're going to get it all together. To hell with half measures! Our goal now is 100 per cent enforceability, and let the paranoia fall where it may. Go after those debts be they one dollar or a million. Go to San Sebastian or Samoa or Sambal V, if need be, and don't worry about the costs. We're following a principle now, and principles are always impractical. Boys, we're overthrowing the reality principle. So get out there and collect all of those debts and groove on completions." '

'His speech is definitely late 1960s,' said the robot. 'Whereas this is the year 2138, or thereabouts. Somebody is conning somebody.'

'Fuck off,' snarled the author.

'That was the call to arms,' the bill collector disguised as a tree said. 'And that is why I am in Harmonia, Mr Mishkin. I have come here, as the result of one man's vision, to collect your debts regardless of time, trouble, and expense.'

'I still can't believe this,' Mishkin said.

'And, yet, there it is. I have a consolidation statement here for everything, Mr Mishkin. Would you care to pay without fuss, or do you want me to get nasty?'

'What debts are you talking about?' Mishkin asked.

'To begin with, there is the matter of your back taxes, Federal, State, and City. Didn't quite get around to paying them last year, did you, Mr Mishkin?'

'It was a tough year.'

'You owe eight thousand seven hundred and fifty-three dollars and fifty-one cents to your Uncle Sammy. Then there is the matter of child support. Sorta passed up on that for a year or so, didn't you, Mishkin? Well, it's a neat four-figure bundle that you owe to poor, abandoned Marcia and little Zelda. Marcia has a new boyfriend, by the way, and little Zelda just flunked out of the Little Red School

House. Marcia asked me to tell you that she is well, having the best time of her life, and wants every cent you owe her, right now, or she'll have you into The Tombs so fast it'll make your teeth spin. She adds that, through psychoanalysis, she finally has the ego strength to tell you that you were always a lousy lay and that everybody breaks up when she relates how diffidently you tried to pursue perversions.'

'That sounds like Marcia,' Mishkin said.

'Next, you owe Marty Bargenfield a thousand dollars. He's your best friend, in case you don't remember. Or he was. I mean, *he* still feels the same, but you've unaccountably cooled off. One might even say that you are avoiding him. Yet, his only crime was to loan you money in a moment of need when you were breaking up with Marcia and had to buy an abortion for Monique.'

'How is Monique?' Mishkin asked.

'She's doing very nicely without you. She is back in Paris, working as a salesgirl in Galeries Lafayette. She still treasures the eighty-cent string of wooden beads that was your only present to her during a tumultuous four-month romance that you have described as "the most moving of my life".'

'I was broke,' Mishkin said. 'And, anyhow, she always said she hated gifts.'

'But you knew better, hey, Mishkie? Never mind, I am not standing in judgement over you. The fact that your conduct, judged by any system of ethics you care to name, makes me want to puke is entirely a personal matter with me and need not concern you at all. Now we come to the Bauhaus Drugstore, at 31 Barrow Street, run by fat, friendly Charlie Ducks, who sold you Dexamyl spansules, Dexadrine tablets, Librium, Carbitol, Nembutal, Seconal, Doriden, and so on, in astonishing quantities during your drug years, all of them on the basis of one non-refillable prescription for phenobarbital – who continued to do so until two years ago when the heat got too hot and he went back to selling Excedrin and lipsticks, and whom you ripped off for one hundred and eighty-six dollars.'

'He cleaned up on me,' Mishkin said. 'He charged me double for everything.'

'You always knew that. Did you ever complain about it?'

'Anyhow, I'm going to pay him as soon as I have some money.'

'But there's never enough money for last year's drugs, eh, Mish? We've all been down that road, baby; but it *is* loathsome, isn't it?'

'I can explain everything,' Mishkin said. 'I have a statement that I would like to read into the record. The facts are capable of various interpretations. I only need a moment to pull my self together.'

The robot extruded an axe from his left hand. He stepped forward and briskly chopped down the bill collector, who perished miserably.

'But I was just about to explain,' Mishkin said.

'Never explain anything,' the robot told him. 'Avoid bummers. Don't go on other people's trips.'

'What is my trip?' Mishkin asked.

'That would be telling,' said the robot.

31 Using Phenomena for Fun

Enjoy a visit to the phenomenal world!

Have a *human* experience – the most fascinating of all experiences.

Now you, too, can experience carnal love, unjustified rage, bad faith. You, too, can know boredom, ennui, angst, accidie.

Thrill to the experience of your 'life' slowly draining away! Feel the inevitable 'death', which you 'know' to be a plunge into pure 'nothingness'.

Live a life of contradictions! Have a wife and lust for other women; possess them and never know satisfaction.

Have children – and feel anxiety, love, hate.

Learn how to be concerned about *possessions*! Worry about your job; identify yourself with what you own.

Feel cowardice!

Derange your senses with drugs!

Live the waking sleep of mortality, lit with uneasy flashes of 'something else'.

Experience the poignancy of wanting a 'better life', and striving for it, and never achieving it.

Be swayed by external and internal stimuli. Be a passive receptor who is acted upon by forces beyond his control.

Have convictions, beliefs, likes and dislikes – for no rational reason!

Feel the intoxication of faith! Thrill to the passion of religion! Apply now!

No Angels under the age of 20,000 years will be allowed into the phenomenal world without written permission from God.

32

'Don't take any more of that dream medicine,' the Life Systems Total Support Mechanism told Mishkin. 'Use me, instead. I am good, useful, beautiful, docile. And you never have to worry about my breaking down and ceasing to function.'

'Do you mean that you never break down?' Mishkin asked.

'That would be an impossible claim. All created things are subject to damage and disrepair. Nothing is immune from breakdown. The important question to be asked is, how are the breakdowns handled?'

'Well, how are they handled?' Mishkin asked.

'In my case,' the LSTSM said, 'I possess a set of interlocking infinite-backup repair systems. If I suffer damage I immediately repair myself, utilizing the most appropriate system. If the appropriate system itself is damaged I automatically shift over to another system.'

'Your number of repair systems is finite, though, isn't it?' Mishkin asked.

'Of course. But the possible combinations and recombinations of my systems and subsystems is large enough to justify the word 'infinite'.

'Amazing,' Mishkin said.

'Yes, I am an uncanny bit of machinery and quite perfect for your needs. I can take care of myself. All I desire is to serve.'

'What is it exactly that you do?'

'I can fry eggs, wash clothes, accompany myself on the banjo – to name but a few of my talents.'

'Everything about you sounds marvellous,' Mishkin said. 'I'll think about it. But now I have to point out that your right front tyre is flat.'

'Damn,' said the LSTSM. 'How embarrassing.'

'But I suppose you can fix it with your infinite-backup repair systems?'

'I'm afraid not,' said the LSTSM. 'It's an unaccountable lapse on the part of my designers. Damn! Back to the old drawing board.'

'I'm sorry,' said Mishkin.

'I am, too,' said the LSTSM. 'We could have been quite perfect for each other if you hadn't been so absurdly choosy.'

The LSTSM turned without another word and limped away through the forest, looking frail, pathetic, and a little funny. Just then three leaves fell from a nearby tree.

33 Spread and Proliferation of Subassemblies

Orchidius had observed everything. Mishkin asked him what he thought about it all.

'There's only one part I didn't understand,' said Orchidius.

'What part was that?'

'That was when the three leaves fell. Why did they do that just at that particular moment?'

'Coincidence,' suggested Mishkin.

'I have heard machines speak and animals answer,' said Orchidius. 'People come and go mysteriously, yet with definite signs of hidden purpose. There is a meaning in everything. But three leaves falling, just then, just there! Who ever heard of such a thing?'

'Personally, I'm more interested in marvels,' Mishkin said.

'I am, too,' said Orchidius. 'We simply disagree on what a marvel is.'

'What are you looking for?' Mishkin asked.

'I really don't know,' Orchidius said. 'But I expect to know intuitively when I find it. What are you looking for?'

'I can't remember,' Mishkin said. 'But I think I'll know it when I see it.'

'Perhaps it's best not to know,' Orchidius said. 'Knowing what you're looking for interferes with your looking for it.'

'I don't think that can be so,' Mishkin said.

'Do you think it's a delusion?' Orchidius asked eagerly. 'I've always wanted to have a genuine delusion.'

The robot was unable to keep silent any longer. 'I've never heard such frivolity in my life.'

'I suppose that frivolity is also a permissible path to salvation?' Orchidius said mildly. 'Whether it is or not, it is the path I'm on. And now my search leads me elsewhere. Good day, gentlemen.'

At the edge of the forest Mishkin and the robot came to a hut with a crude sign over the door reading, INN OF THE FOUR WINDS. And there to greet them, wearing a shirt of homespun and leather bells, was Orchidius.

Mishkin expressed amazement at seeing his friend in this place, the evident owner of an inn; but Orchidius told him that it was the most natural thing in the world. He told how he had come to this place, tired and thirsty, but above all hungry. He had gathered herbs and vegetables and made a soup, and then he trapped a rabbit and made a stew.

People came by, tired and thirsty, but above all hungry. Orchidius shared his stew with them, and they helped him to build a hut. Others came by and Orchidius fed them, and sometimes they would not, or could not, pay, but usually they could and would, in one way or another. It seemed quite natural to them that there should be an inn here, at this place and no other, and that Orchidius should be running it. It never occurred to them that Orchidius was just passing through, like them, and that perhaps he, too, had other places to go to and other duties to attend to. They thought that he was a natural and necessary part of the scenery, since they believed that inns should be found wherever people needed them and that, according to universal law, every inn had to be equipped with an innkeeper.

After a while Orchidius came to accept this view. He advertised for a chambermaid. He complained that the quality of rabbits had fallen off. He suspected everyone of being an inspector from the *Guide Michelin.* He planned to expand his inn, to buy a soft ice-cream maker, to get a franchise from Howard Johnson's, to plant palm trees and illuminate them with hidden lights. He began to worry about fuel bills and taxes. He raised his prices for high season and offered specials for low season.

'But how did you get into all of that?' Mishkin asked.

'It seemed plausible at the time,' Orchidius answered. 'It still seems plausible.'

'I want a single room with a bath,' Mishkin said. 'And a tank of gas for my robot.'

'Regular or special?' Orchidius asked. Then he burst into tears. He wrote a note that read, 'This inn is closed while its owner continues his Trip.' He nailed the note to the door and left at once for parts unknown, taking nothing with him but a battery-operated television set and a pair of gold clubs.

34

Mishkin and the robot also resumed their journey. They passed a tree upon which were carved the words, 'Orchidius was here in person on his Trip'.

Carved on another tree: 'This Trip is the property of Orchidius'.

And on another: 'Everybody is a bit player in the movie of Orchidius's life'.

'We seem to meet quite often,' Mishkin said. 'Do you suppose that we are the same person?'

'Definitely not,' said Orchidius. 'You are logical and realistic and goal-oriented, and you have a personality and a history and even a few character traits, whereas I am an abstraction who just slips in and out of things for no reason and no purpose.'

'My trip is overdetermined,' Mishkin said. 'It's also freaky. Too much is happening to me. I can't stand the changes.'

'I can't stand them, either. Maybe we're going about things in the wrong way.'

The robot said, 'You are both going about things in the right way and you're both simultaneously the same person and different people and you're both on the same trip even though your trips aren't the same.'

'Can you explain what all of that means?' Mishkin asked.

'No, I can't,' the robot said. 'Robots are allowed only a small supply of wisdom, and I have used up all of mine for at least a week.'

All that week the robot could barely put one foot after another. He was incapable of oiling himself, couldn't finish the simplest task, and his answers to even the simplest questions were ridiculous in the extreme.

At the end of the week he was recovered and ready to explain what all of that had meant. But Mishkin didn't ask him. Mishkin liked to have his meals cooked properly and his clothes washed promptly. He thought it was no bargain to exchange a good servant for a sage of dubious qualifications. The robot himself offered no protest.

35 The Doctor of Juxtapositions

'Great Scott, MacGregor, I believe that in some unaccountable fashion we have passed through an obverse transverse of the space-time continuum and have actually *returned to Earth* and that we are now viewing everything through altered topological ratios, thus causing subtle changes in our perception of received reality!!!'

36 Festival of the Mind

Special techniques, reawaken!

Hypnotize yourself into becoming yourself. Energize your

Receptive Centre. Shut off signals from the uptight old Censor. Give yourself suggestions. Give yourself autosuggestions. Give yourself automatic autosuggestions. New technique of 'flagging' the subconscious allows you to give yourself automatic subconscious autosuggestions *without your even knowing about it!*

Go beyond drugs into experiences that simulate the drug simulations of experiences that can be achieved only by Higher Consciousness.

Enjoy sexual intercourse in your sleep without a partner.

Process the computer power in your mind: you can do it/it can do you.

READOUT IS INSIGHT READOUT IS INSIGHT
READOUT IS INSIGHT

Magi for sale or rent: plump Hindu Master, speaking incomprehensible prehensile English, has turban, will travel. Chinese Master with inscrutable smile and acupuncture kit never believed in communism, must travel. British Master specializing in discipline – 'mental restraint is the road to freedom' – doesn't believe in socialism, listens to acid rock. American Master, AC-DC, doesn't believe in anything for very long – teaches the communal road to rugged individualism – has large supply of mandalas, mantras, yantras – uses rational mysticism to achieve mind-blowing pragmatic effects – disarming, boyish smile – wears fringed leather pants – doesn't believe in law of cause and effect but pays taxes anyhow – rates 35.2 on the schizophrenia machine – sexually liberated, except when anxious . . .

Orchidius was at the Festival of the Mind. He wore a headband, robe, and sandals, and employed hieratic gestures of great power and economy. He had his own booth and for two days gave prophecies with fair success but on the third day reverted to a previous imprinting and turned his booth into a hot dog stand.

Mishkin wandered through the Festival and ate cotton candy and thought bittersweet thoughts of his youth, just like everyone else. He smiled politely and disdainfully, just like everybody else. But this was no real indication of his true attitude. Mishkin was a secret pilgrim. He wanted out of his bag, out of repetition-compulsion, out of confusion, out of tedious novelty. Just like everybody else.

When does the ecstasy begin?

37 Magus Reveals Secrets

Q. The approach to enlightenment involves an apparent contradiction, which is exemplified in the dual personality of the con-man sage. The problem is always the same: Why did the leader betray us? Did he find us unworthy? Or was the betrayal a secret act of love done in order to let us work out the final stage of our destinies on our own? Or did the leader's powers fail? Or could it be that he never had any power at all? Which story are we stuck in?

A. Perhaps it's a case of divine ambiguities: the complications pile up, everything modifies everything else, vagueness is king. Would you like that story? Or how about ambiguity for fun and profit – the magus. He is putting you on. You're doing numbers over the divine spirituality of it all, and he's laughing up his embroidered sleeve, not very nice. Is *that* the story you'd prefer?

Q. What's going on around here? Why isn't anything working out?

A. Should I take you by the hand? Very well, but where will I lead you? Of course, I could put it all in order, and we could dance a minuet. I do want to amuse you, but really, there's a limit. Do you really want a guided tour through the formal gardens promised in the prospectus? Maybe that would be OK for you, but how about me? I'm supposed to have some fun, too. But now I'm starting to sound like a reform rabbi, and I notice that Mishkin has just gotten himself into a sort of interesting situation, so let's look into the house on Willow Road and see what is happening.

38

'But Professor Mackintosh, how do you know it is Earth that we have finally returned to?'

The professor smiled softly and pointed with his cane. 'Do you see that flower over there? It is *Hemerocallis fulva*, known as the day lily, and common throughout much of the United States. Those orange-coloured blossoms open but for a single day, you know – not proof positive, but rather good circumstantial evidence – like a trout in the milk, as Thoreau said.'

39

Mishkin clung to the outer edges of the face, which began to melt, the nose flattening and segueing into the cheek, the eyes bleeding into the hair, the mouth softening and blurring, the handholds pulling out of the silly putty, and Mishkin slid away through obligatory swallow song, and long, still Ohio nights with the crickets raucous in the box-berry hedges, and the telephone lines black against the sky like a diagram of your whole life.

It was like that, but it wasn't exactly like that. It was more like those hushed summer nights in the old frame house in Rushmore, Mississippi, when an intolerable sweetness clung to the moist denim stretched over a young girl's sleeping buttocks, and you realized, young though you were, that things were going to happen to you, and you would live by them and lose by them, but always, somewhere, the river would wind, dark and sinuous, sweet mother of the past, companion of the present, mourner of the irretrievable future.

A slingshot. With this weapon Mishkin shot his way through innumerable fantasies. Later, he exchanged his slingshot for an M-1 and shot his way through the same fantasies.

An empty butter wrapper. Mishkin once ate an entire pound of butter at a single sitting, washing it down with a quart of ice-cold milk. Now he lives away from home and picks at his food like a bird.

An Indian war club. Mishkin made this at camp. He also made Mary Lou Watkins at the same camp but not all the way. Later on Mishkin made a lot of people all the way. Now he travels.

A page of sheet music entitled 'Old Black Joe'. Mishkin didn't think about Negroes when he was a boy. Now, a man, he doesn't think about blacks. But he talks about them and dreams about them.

A snapshot of Mishkin's mother at the age of twenty-three. Mishkin thinks he doesn't care very much about his mother. Mishkin also thinks he doesn't con himself very much.

A Sanskrit grammar. Mishkin once planned to learn Sanskrit in order to read *The Upanishads* in the original. Now he doesn't even read them in English.

41

Mishkin ascended to heaven on a fiery chariot and there he met the Lord God of Hosts, and Mishkin prostrated himself before the Deity and said, 'Lord, Lord, I have sinned,' which seemed a pretty good thing to say under the circumstances.

But God smiled and raised Mishkin up and said, 'Rather, Mishkin, say that I have sinned; for what are your sins but the deficiencies that I caused to be put into you in order to test you and give you grievous trials and a dark night of the soul, the point being that you should overcome them. This may seem a kind of weird way of operating, but it is unreservedly recommended on page 102 of the best seller, *This Business of Being God*, written by a symposium of Parisian intellectuals and American hippies, and published by the Godhead Institution with offices in New York, London, Paris, Ibiza, and Katmandu, and with a foreword by Yours Truly.'

'I have failed the crucial tests,' Mishkin said. 'I am mean, nasty, greedy, selfish, and uncaring.'

'Don't get into a masochism number,' said God. 'Just as there is love which surpasseth understanding, so there is understanding which surpasseth love. For have I not written, the last shall be the first?'

'You are kind,' Mishkin said. 'But I don't really understand.'

'Understanding is a down,' God said. 'Be comforted, Mishkin, for your vibrations are OK, and I think right now I need a vacation.'

'I think,' Mishkin said, 'that it is time for a bit of static description. And then a bit of action.' The space fleet came thundering in on fiery jets. Somewhere, a tree was crying. Mishkin's father said, 'Maybe I don't know what I like, but I sure as shooting know what I don't like.' The people next door were a mystery, according to Angela. 'Take nothing into account.' 'But what do you mean, a mystery?' Claire couldn't explain, but she felt it was time for a bit of static description, and then a bit of action. 'It doesn't really *work* that way.' Mishkin knew that it was true and untrue, and he loved her and hated her for it. It was a complicated world, but so what?

Mishkin liked a bit of complication : 'Excuse me, Captain, the pusher beam trigger mechanism seems to have broken down.' But not too much. He liked story lines that you could follow while thinking of other things. 'Spare me that avant-garde stuff,' Alice said, 'besides, it's not your thing.' Not my thing? Then why bother building palaces out of frying pans, why look for a jewel on the forehead of a toad? Subjects and verbs must agree, everyone agreed, but not on anything else.

Mishkin wondered what a spaceship looked like. What could you compare a spaceship to? Itself? 'The spaceship looked utterly like itself.' Jane shook her head. Mishkin's father shook his head. Mishkin tried to play the flute. His skin itched. He wished he could think of something a spaceship looked like. Not itself. He decided to buy a toy spaceship and describe that.

43 Specialist Lists Eye Osmosis as Primary Cause of Possession

Mishkin's eye fastened itself upon the sight and became what it saw. The eye is a powerful organ of adaptation. Mishkin is also a powerful organ of adaptation. Mishkin's eye had been cursed, and now, seeing crabgrass and hard boiled eggs, it became what it beheld.

44 Doctor Mishkin Operates

Mishkin touched the young girl's head with an exploratory gesture. Then, swiftly, he turned up the two tabs and separated the halves of the skull. From within he drew out a printed circuit board. Soon he saw the damage and repaired it with professional competence, noting the work on the inventory list pasted to the inside of the left hemisphere of the skull. Then he put the two halves of the skull back together, taking care to bend the tabs carefully into place. The girl blinked her eyes and awakened, cured of her nervous tic and nocturnal enuresis.

45 Premature Conclusions

Poor Ramsey Davis was impaled upon an ornamental iron railing at Thirteenth and Fifth. Of sweet, shy Marguerite Onger, less is known; she was last seen spiralling into the Arctic behind a howling dog pack, herself howling, the dogs saying to each other, 'Wow, freaky scene, man, like get me out of here.' Young David Broomsley died fever-twitched with clumsy face appalled. Mishkin himself was turned into a turnip by a malignant magician and inadvertently eaten by Richard Southey of Charing Cross Road. Ormsley never died and is still living in San Miguel de Allende, but his nose is in traction due to a rather unusual car accident. Orchidius is serving a ten-year sentence for mail fraud at Fulsome Prison. He swears he is innocent, and money to help his appeal should be sent to the author, care of the publisher, and I'll do what I can to assist this unfortunate man. Various creatures in this work died in various ways. The author of this work would like to go out snarling but will probably be reduced to snuffling. Peace be to all, and to all a good night.

46

Mishkin loped gracefully along the contours of his life, stopping now and again to change into levis, suede pants, black bandit hats, and pausing to eat an unscheduled pizza here and there. Mishkin, slit-eyed against the wind of time, faintly smiling Mishkin, nerves twitching in the long, cold jaw, hard hands set on dream steering wheels. Prince of jesters, Mishkin, with his clown's grin and his errand boy mendacity. Was he not disastrous, unscheduled? Mishkin, of the bright, fey smile and winsome ways, dappling his way through all his completions. Mishkin in there for the big fifty-cent ride of all the amusements, holding on to his identity for dear life as the merry-go-round swirled his images about like dead leaves. Mishkin pretended to be who he was.

47

Mishkin sat in the Memory Theatre and scratched his crotch. On the stage, brilliantly lighted, a tableau appeared : a woman holding a baby. Mishkin recognized them as his own. A great voice called out, 'What do you feel, Mishkin?' And Mishkin replied, 'I feel an itch in my crotch. Also, I have a feeling that I forgot to file this year's income tax.'

Acid is an intensifier. Soap is an emulsifier. Take your choice.

If you don't dig chromosome damage buy better chromosomes.

I used to be afraid that I was going out of my mind. Now I am afraid that I am not going out of my mind.

48

Dear Tom,

Thought I'd write you a letter, old buddy, learn how you are and fill you in on how it goes with yours truly and friends and company. Remember Martha? Well, she's gone and done it again but this time with a giant topaz on display at the Islamic Museum in Trebizond, of all places. Agnes has had another lamination, and more power to her, I say. Your little nephew Felix has been elected to a full term as Master of the neo-Eleusinian Mysteries. They say he's clairvoyant plus, but I say it's absurd to expose a little boy to those obscenities. *Alleged* obscenities, since I'm not supposed to know anything about it.

Local news : synchronicity has staged another comeback, and people are wandering all over in search of 'serendipitous events and adventitious objects'. Schenley's Square Face Acid is still the workingman's potion. It renders them inefficient, which is all to the good. And so on and so on and so on.

As for me, I'm doing as well as can be expected. I entered the Game late, and I still have a lot of malimprinting to overcome. I have been able to master primary life systems, however, despite the dire predictions of Mr Chang. So now I can take over my own involuntary musculature. Total nerve control is still tough, however, and sometimes I think I'll simply junk the whole thing and go sit under a tree.

There are a lot of saints around, as always, and most of them smell bad, as always. There's no accounting for fads.

Well, that's all the local news that I can think of just now, and I want to get this out to you in a hurry. I still don't know why you've picked an exterior adventure rather than an interior one. Soft spot in the old psyche? Or are you pulling a reverse on us, you sly dog? It would be just like you to manifest a simple little ext. adv. spaceflight and then fool us by plunging into the pit of unmitigated self! (But if that's the case, how did you find the interface? Or are you pulling a double reverse? The 'mind' boggles.)

I'll just assume that you've chosen a complex way of getting into (or out of) Maya and that there's no need for me to remind you of the pitfalls and perils involved, since you know more than I do about mirror-deformations in the theatre of self. Of course, I just now *have* reminded you; but I don't mean to be insulting, I know that even the greatest adepts can profit from the words of a fool.

Your wives have remarried, as you must have foreseen. Some of your children have changed their names, which maybe you didn't expect. But then, maybe you expected everything.

Yours,
Otto

49 Do Not Fill in Separations

These apparent discontinuities have been devised and implanted for your own safety and welfare. Please do not connect them with 'logical' links. This sort of premature closure would spoil their facticity, and would result in a dangerous – perhaps fatal – state of accidie for you. Extreme perceptual looseness is recommended. Remember that low-level scanning is the key to total field perception.

Thank you,
John Macpherson,
Commissioner, Dept of Public Mental Hygiene

50 Whispering Voices

'Repetition is inevitable.'

'Proceed by separations.'

'Is someone trying to tell you something?'

'Read reversals.'

'Distortions must be expected.'

51 Reminder

Mishkin saw a tape recorder on stilts. He went over and turned it on. The recorder said: 'This is a recorded message to remind you not to forget to record a message to remind you not to forget.'

52

'Yep, sonny, it's quite a sight – the biggest cause and effect factory in the whole danged galaxy. Works simple enough. We put the causes into this hopper and the effects into this hopper. Then the machinery takes over, and there's a lot of clanging and banging, and the product comes out over here – a nicely bonded cause-and-effect without a single seam visible to the naked eye. Our cause-and-effect bonds will stand up in any court of law anywhere.

'We don't have no truck with them newfangled ideas about discontinuity and synchronicity and all that crap. Around here, if a horse kicks you, you get a broken leg, and if you've got a bellyache it's because you ate Italian sausage last night. That way everybody knows where they stand.'

'Well, damnation, I don't know why a thing like that had to go and happen. Still, sometimes it does happen. Sometimes a cause and effect absolutely refuse to bond. When that happens, and we ain't got no explanation for something, we call it God's Will. So I guess it was God's Will that this happened now with you, and I think we should kneel down for a moment of silent prayer.'

53

Mishkin came to a long line of men. The man on the extreme left was listening to a transistor radio tuned very low. He heard something, turned to the man on his right, whispered, 'You only live once. Pass it on.'

54

Tom Mishkin and James Bradley Sooner sat down to the meal. The mouse jumped on to the table and began lugging plates around, serving mashed potatoes, cutting the roast beef. Mishkin asked, 'Does he always do that?'

The mouse said, 'I will admit that it is a curious situation. Allow me to explain. For one thing, I am Jewish. For another . . .'

'Serve the goddamned food!' Sooner roared.

'Don't get so excited,' the mouse said and went back to work.

'Now, about this strange thing that happened to me,' Sooner said.

55

The player drew three cards and threw down his hand in disgust. 'I came into this game with no stake and lousy cards,' he said, 'but this draw is simply the end.' He pulled a revolver from his pocket and shot himself in the head.

Another man moved into his place, picked up his hand, grinned, and bet his life.

Speckled landscape. The whitebird of bitterness. White eyes. White legs. Whiteout.

Like the man who set fire to his friend's overcoat upon hearing the command, 'Light up a Chesterfield'.

SILVER SWANS SWAP SOPHISTRIES

56

'How long do the hallucinations go on?' Mishkin asked.

'Not long enough.'

'What is this?' Mishkin asked.

'This,' Orchidius said, 'is a device for altering reality.'

The object was the size and shape of an ostrich's egg. It had a single toggle switch. One side was marked, 'On'. The other side was marked, 'Off'. The switch was turned to 'Off'.

'Where did you get it?'

'I bought it at the Whole Earth Store,' Orchidius said. 'It cost $9.95.'

'Does it really alter reality?'

'It's supposed to. I haven't tried it yet.'

'How could it?' Mishkin asked. 'How could anything alter reality for $9.95?'

'At that price it sounded too good to pass up,' Orchidius said. 'But I guess it can't work.'

'You can't be sure,' Mishkin said. 'You haven't tried it yet.'

'I don't suppose it's really necessary to try it,' Orchidius said.

'Of course it is! Push the switch!'

'You push it.'

'All right, I'll push it.' Mishkin took the egg and pushed the switch 'On'. They both waited for several seconds.

'Nothing happened,' Orchidius said.

'I guess not. But how would we know it if something did happen? I mean, whatever happened would still seem like reality to us.'

'That's true.'

'Maybe you'd better turn it off.'

'Turn what off?' Sooner asked.

58

The heroic figure of a man, holding a flute in one hand, a serpent in the other. This man says, 'Enter.'

A horned woman mounted on a werewolf, holding a sickle in one hand, a pomegranate in the other. This woman takes your overcoat.

A man with a jackal's head, naked except for winged sandals. In one hand he holds a fragment of papyrus, in the other a bronze disc. This man says, 'Immediate seating in the first three rows.'

How many more reminders could anyone want?

59

Puzzle picture: Concealed in this rustic landscape is God. The first viewer who correctly identifies himself will receive, at absolutely no cost to himself, satori. Second prize is a weekend at Grossingers.

60

'How long will the hallucinations continue?' Mishkin asked.

'What hallucinations?'

61

Mishkin, at the age of twelve, loved God so greatly that he broke his marriage vows to himself.

Mishkin was unfaithful to himself again today, preferring the affections of a stylish sports car and a suede jacket to the ardent constancy and unstinting love of Mishkin.

'Your problem,' the analyst said, 'is an inability to love yourself.'

'But I do love myself!' Mishkin declared. 'I do! I really do!'

'Do you expect me to believe that?' the analyst asked. 'I saw you looking at Sartre, Camus, Montaigne, Plato, Thoreau – to mention only a few of your lights o' love. When will you stop having these absurd, incessant, and unrewarding affairs?'

'I love myself,' Mishkin wept. 'I really do.'

'Still smoking,' the analyst noted. 'Still lethargic, passive, uncontrolled. Is this the way you treat one whom you claim to love?'

62

Deep in the woods, Mishkin found an apostrophe. It was lost and crying softly to itself. Mishkin took it in his arms and stroked its soft fur. The apostrophe sank its curved claws into Mishkin's shoulder. Mishkin ignored the pain and continued to smoke his cigarette.

They took his card and punched it. At once he felt relief, and then boredom, and then anxiety. He felt fine as soon as they put a new card into his hand.

The footprints continued into the woods. Mishkin followed them. He was well armed, prepared to face the fabulous beast. At last he saw it ahead of him and hastily fired. Too late he realized that he had shot one of his avatars. The avatar expired. Mishkin felt a sense of loss that became, inevitably, a sense of relief.

63 The Sorrows of the Man of a Thousand Disguises

The Man of a Thousand Disguises sat in his temporary office and considered the problem of Mishkin and the engine part. Somehow, the two would not come together, the desired juxtaposition would not come off. There was no flow towards the desired objective.

Because of the difficulties inherent in this problem, The Man had been forced to invent himself – a *deus ex machina* – now standing tongue-tied in front of the audience and endeavouring to explain what was to himself still inexplicable.

Having constructed himself, The Man of a Thousand Disguises was now stuck with himself. Did he also have to explain himself? Quickly, he abolished the necessity for doing so. He only had to explain about how Mishkin and the engine part came together. But how in fact *did* they come together? Did they really have to?

'And so they came to their untimely ends, Mishkin, the cosmic jester, and the engine part, which was the cruel and paradoxical point of his joke. Yes, they perished, and at the same time the Earth fell into the sun, the sun blew up, and the entire galaxy fell through a black hole in the fabric of space-time, thus obliterating the tragi-comedy of human existence, and indeed, all dramas, all existences.'

No, delicious though it was, it simply wouldn't do. Mishkin and his engine part had to get together, the original problem had to be solved, all promises and premises had to be kept. After that was done, everything could be blown up but not before.

So there it was again: The Man of a Thousand Disguises still had the unhappy duty of accomplishing the job for which he had created himself.

He thought. Nothing intruded upon his disastrous solitude. Stray conceptions clouded his mind: 'Any drug that fucks you up is good'. 'Depression is inevitable'. 'Concomitants'. 'Paris'.

With an effort The Man forced his attention towards the engine part. Where was the damned thing now? In some dusty warehouse on Earth, presumably, awaiting extrication for the delectation of the patient reader.

'But who needs a reader who's a patient?' The Man snarled. Nevertheless, there it was: He was under contractual obligation to himself to construct a ballet for catatonics.

The Man tried to pull himself together. 'I am losing my mind.' 'Nonexistent problems have the maximum reality.' 'Not exactly what we had in mind.'

How true it was! People who live in glass psyches shouldn't cast words.

To work: The Man of a Thousand Disguises picked up his analogic slide rule and inferential stylus. Now then: engine part become eagle heart, standing start, running water, ice. So much for the J series. Again now: treasure in the earth, crystal goblet, lathe, laughter, bat, slink, reduction gear.

More like it!

Moving with more confidence now, The Man put all the available data into the recycler and let it stand for three revolutions. Then he pressed the Outcome button. Up came an antelope mounted on a polar bear. Worthless! But wait a minute now – *polar bear* – yes, it's coming: *polarity bears ante lope!* A yin function breach delivery, definitely productive.

Now to put it all through the constructs simulator.

Johnny Allegro was feeling out of sorts that morning. He set the derby on his black glossy hair. Carefully, he straightened the cuffs of his chocolate mohair shirt. Now he was ready for business.

The telephone rang. Allegro pounced on it. 'Allegro speaking.'

'Johnny? This is Harry van Orlen.'

Allegro pictured the big-bellied, slack-jawed gunman with the heavily stubbled jaws and the grimy fingernails.

'Well, what is it?' Johnny snapped. He hated cheap gunsels, even though his work frequently required him to spend eighteen hours a day with them.

'It's like this, Johnny. Do you remember that job we did on South Main Street?'

'Yeah,' Johnny snarled, recognizing at once the euphemism referring to the recent burglary of the Wel-Rite Storage Company on Varick Street.

'Well, we found buyers for all the inventory except one piece of hardware we're still stuck with.'

'What kind of a product is it?' Johnny asked.

'It's some sort of gadget labelled Spaceship Engine Part L-1223A. It was supposed to be sent to some guy named Mishkin in some place called Harmonia.'

'So, sell it.'

'Nobody wants it.'

'Then dump it somewhere.' Johnny slammed down the telephone, scowling. He hated it when his underlings bothered him with questions that an ape would be able to solve while going downhill on roller skates. But he also hated unwarranted initiative.

Just then a thought occurred to him: Maybe he should

send that engine part to that guy, what was his name, that Mishkin, thus acquiring for himself the reputation of an eccentric philanthropist. Then he could do a few more nice things and maybe after that run for elected office.

This notion suited Johnny's strange notions of *noblesse oblige*. He reached for the telephone.

Just then the door burst open and three policemen and an author burst into the room with drawn guns.

Johnny snarled in rage. His lightning-quick reflexes enabled him to dive beneath the desk before the policemen's bullets ripped through the space where he had just been.

'Get him!' screamed the author. 'He knows where the part is!'

But Johnny had already pushed the blue button under his desk. A section of floor opened under him and Johnny fell through a chute that led to the garage where his Mercedes SL 300 was waiting, its motor ticking over quietly.

65

Some days later, on the cool, raffia-covered veranda of the large, weather-beaten house on lower Key Largo, Professor John O. MacAllister was undergoing a moment of severe perplexity. This was unusual for the tall, strongly built, sandy-haired physicist from Rockport, Maine. Beside him was Lois, his tall, attractive, chestnut-haired wife. She had just entered the veranda.

Before Lois had a chance to speak, towheaded Tyie Oliver ran up on to the cool veranda with a five ball in his hand. 'Pool, anyone?' he asked fatuously.

'Not just now, Tyie,' said Professor MacAllister in quiet tones.

Tyie turned to go. But then it became apparent, even to his untrained and unobservant eye, that there was something strange and unnatural in the bearing of the two people he had known for only a month but already prized more than anyone in the world.

'Is anything the matter?' Tyie asked.

Before anyone could answer, Lois MacAllister's younger sister, Patty, came down the inner steps and out on to the veranda. Not yet seventeen, Patty was singularly developed for her age. She sat down in a faded green armchair and crossed the long, generously curved legs that fell from the slender waist below her ample and delicately shaped breasts.

'Yes, John,' she said, tart-sweet, '*is* anything the matter?'

Professor MacAllister went a shade pale beneath the healthy glow of his tan. He noted that his wife's grey eyes had widened. Quietly, he said, 'Now, wait just a minute . . .'

The kitchen door opened. Out on to the veranda came Chang, the Chinese cook, Kyoto, the Philippine houseboy, and Mary Lou, the Jamaican housekeeper. They ranged themselves silently along the wall. And now it was Patty's turn to go pale.

There was a long silence. Then Tyie said, 'Uh, I guess I'd better be getting home. The paint on the birdcage is probably dry by now, and I . . .'

'Don't rush away, Tyie,' said Lois MacAllister. "There's someone here I think you should meet.'

The cellar door opened and out on to the veranda came a bald, one-eyed dwarf, a thin man in a black suit, and a pair of giggling, blonde, female twins.

'Now I think we can clear this thing up,' MacAllister said. 'First, as to the so-called mysterious package that Ed Whittaker found in the bilge of the garbage scow, *Clotilda*, just two days before his disappearance ...'

'Yes?' Patty breathed.

'It contained nothing more than an engine part for a spaceship. It was supposed to be sent to a Mr Mishkin of Harmonia, and in the presence of Judge Clarke I forwarded it to the Dade County Emergency Expediting Service.'

Patty slumped back, her body slack with relief. 'Well, that takes care of that! We've all been a pack of fools!'

'Maybe,' said Lois MacAllister. 'But we still haven't heard any explanation for the rest of it.'

Professor MacAllister looked thoughtfully at the people on the veranda. 'That,' he said, 'may take a little longer.' He went to the sideboard and poured himself a drink.

66

The sign on the door read : CONTINUITIES, INC. Uncle Arnold went inside and was shown to the office of Thomas Grantwell.

'I've come here about my nephew,' Uncle Arnold said. 'Tom Mishkin is his name. He's stranded on a planet called Harmonia, and he's gotta have a certain engine part so's he can make his spaceship run again. But I can't seem to get the part to him.'

'Have you tried shipping it by space freight?' Grantwell asked.

'I have. But they told me that the Interstellar Space Flight Premise had been suspended this year, and therefore they were unable to help me.'

'Did you ask them what was supposed to happen to your nephew?'

'They said that they would provisionally have to deny his existence until the Premise was reinstated.'

'That's government for you,' Grantwell said. 'Leaves you – or rather young Mishkin – in quite a spot.'

'Is there anything your organization can do to help the lad?' asked Uncle Arnold.

'There is,' Grantwell said, firmly. 'Continuities, Inc was designed to create connections between incompatible assumptions. We will design a scenario that will provide a link between these two different realities without doing violence to either.'

'That's wonderful,' Uncle Arnold said.

And so it came to pass that all the toads were smoothed over and various elephants were secretly enlisted. The next step was more severe: suitable gapping material had to be found, heads had to be turned, performances judged. Spontaneity died in Kansas City and was replaced by probity.

Gigantic mechanisms were turned loose upon a suspecting Earth. Various marches were organized. The input factory increased outputs. Crimson dagles carried darkness and invisibility. People decided things. There was a necessary series of transactions conducted via radio and involving a compromise about permissible ratios of feeling.

Nor was this all. The world stood revealed in dark vestments. Certain facts of long-established limpidity died aborning. The strain on the normative cause-and-effect linkages was tremendous. Voices were raised in protest. Outright revolt was threatened.

The author, in the meantime, had formed a dismal awareness of the difficulties involved. He toyed with various possibilities, even considered killing Mishkin off and starting a new book – a cookbook, perhaps. Still ...

67 Peregrinations

'Damn it all,' said Mishkin, 'another zero-null game.'

The engine part could be seen in all its splendour, isolated in the author's mind. It was a hazy visualization, sometimes resembling a pot roast, at other times a Citroën 2 cv. The part sounded like a rock band. It smelt like a butane burner.

68 Certificate of Unreality

Mishkin was resting in a glade. The robot was enjoying a pseudo-rest, since he didn't need a real rest. Mishkin looked up and became aware that someone was striding across the sward towards him.

'Hello, there,' said The Man of a Thousand Disguises. 'I'm in charge of this sequence. I have come here in person to formalize a resolution.'

'What are you talking about?' Mishkin asked. 'I'm just waiting here for a spaceship part.'

The Man grimaced. 'I'm terribly sorry about that, but you see, we are no longer entertaining that premise. The whole conception of you on an alien planet, waiting for a spaceship part – well, it had been declared dramatically unsound. Therefore, we are scrapping it.'

'Does that mean that you are also scrapping me?'

The Man looked at him unhappily. 'Well, yes, I'm afraid that it does. We have found a new hero to take your place.'

THE NEW HERO

He was complicated, devious, terribly attractive, masculine, universal. He had idiosyncracies, habits, traits. He had soul, pzazz, vital juices. He had a sex life. He had a complicated and ambiguous history. He had a little mole to the left of his nose. He had satanic eyebrows. He was a knockout.

'This is your replacement,' said The Man. 'You've done your best, Mishkin. It's no fault of yours if you've gotten into this untenable situation. But really, we must end this thing, and to do that we need some cooperation from our characters, and you – well, you simply don't have any *characteristics* for us to work with.'

Mishkin instantly developed a facial tic, a stammer, a way of biting his lips before and after speaking, a moustache, and a removable false tooth.

'Sorry, it's not quite what we had in mind,' said The Man. 'Now, I will just leave you boys to get acquainted.' The Man turned himself into a tree.

'How do you do?' Mishkin said.

'How do you do?' said Mr Hero.

'Would you care for a nice cup of coffee?' said Mishkin.

'Thanks, that would be nice,' said Mr Hero.

Mishkin poured coffee. They sipped in silence.

Mr Hero said, 'Nice weather we've been having.'

'Where?' Mishkin said.

'Oh, in Limbo,' said Mr Hero. 'I've been waiting there with the other archetypes.'

'It's been nice here, too,' Mishkin said.

The tree changed into The Man. 'Interact!' he hissed and turned into a tree again.

Mr Hero smiled diffidently. 'Rather an awkward situation, isn't it?'

'I suppose it is,' Mishkin said. 'Personally, ever since I started this thing I've been in just one akward situation after another. Maybe a rest would do me good.'

'Yes,' said Mr Hero. 'But before that, it would be terribly good of you to explain the ropes to me. I mean, new man on the job, and all that...' He broke off with an embarrassed laugh.

'Well,' Mishkin said, 'there's not much to explain. You just go along and things happen to you.'

'But that's rather – *passive* – isn't it?'

'Sure, it is. But it's that kind of adventure.'

'What about motivation?' asked Mr Hero.

'As far as I know,' Mishkin said, 'you're looking for a spaceship part.'

'A what?'

'A part to replace a broken part in your spaceship. Without it your spaceship won't run. And that means you can't get back to Earth. And you do want to get back to Earth –

that's an unspoken assumption that I personally think ought to be examined. Anyhow, that's your motivation.'

'I see,' said Mr Hero. 'Not much you can get your *teeth* into, is there?'

'It's no Oedipus Rex,' Mishkin admitted. 'But then, what is?'

Mr Hero chuckled appreciatively. 'That's terribly true, what is, indeed? Well, now, who is this other chap?'

'He's a robot,' Mishkin said.

'Why is he here?'

'I can't remember the original reason. But mainly he's here so that you won't have to talk to yourself.'

Mr Hero looked at the robot apprehensively. 'My mother was raped by a robot,' he remarked. 'That's her story. The robot said that he mistook her for a refrigerator. I've felt dodgy about robots ever since. Is this robot a nice robot?'

The robot looked up. 'Yes,' he said, 'I'm a nice robot, especially when people have the common courtesy to address me as if I am here when I am here, rather than speaking as if I weren't here, which, frankly, the way things are going these days, I'd just as soon rather not be.'

'Prolix, isn't he?' said Mr Hero.

'If you don't like it,' said the robot, 'you can always stuff it up your nose.'

Mr Hero rolled his eyes, then abruptly giggled.

The Man transformed himself from a tree into The Man. 'That's it,' he said. 'I'm sorry, Mr Hero, but you don't seem to be the type we had in mind.'

'So where's that at?' Mr Hero said haughtily. 'Can I help it if you don't know what you're doing?'

'Go back at once to the collective pool of the unconscious,' said The Man.

Mr Hero vanished with hauteur.

'Now we're back where we started from,' Mishkin said.

'That was my line,' the robot said.

'Shut up,' said The Man. 'I gotta think.' He sat down upon a rock – a tall, sombre, light-haired man with a moustache and a terribly attractive way with women. His long, strong fingers rippled as he tapped them on one bony knee. There were dark shadows hiding his smouldering eyes. He was a knockout. But he wasn't happy. No, he wasn't happy. Perhaps he would never be happy. Had not Dr Lifshultz told him once, 'Happiness is just a thing called Joe.' And The Man's name was not Joe. So he was not happiness nor were any of his pursuits or practices.

Part Two

69 And so Once More Into the Breach, Brave Friends

The prau glided over the clear waters of the creek, guided by the deft paddle of the aged Dayak who brought the frail craft expertly alongside the bamboo dock that connected the village of Omandrik with the outside world.

A white man – an American – dressed in mosquito boots, jodhpurs, a sweat-stained white shirt and crushed bush hat, had been watching the arrival of the native craft from the relative coolness of the long-shadowed veranda of his house. He rose without haste and checked the chambers of the .38 calibre Cross & Blackwell revolver that he habitually carried in a well-oiled chamois holster strapped under his right armpit. Then, moving easily through the sultry tropic heat, he shambled down to the pier.

The first man to step off the ancient steamboat was a tall Arab in flowing white robes and a white and yellow head-dress of the Hadhramaut. He was followed by an enormously fat man of indeterminate age, wearing a red fez, a crumpled suit of white silk, and sandals. The fat man might have been taken for Turkish, but a keen observer, noting the faintly slanted green eyes nearly lost in rolls of fat, would have guessed him to be a Hungarian from the Carpathian steppes. He was followed by a short, emaciated, provisional English boy of some twenty years of age, whose over-quick gestures and trembling hands proclaimed a terminal amphetamine user and beneath whose denim jacket might be glimpsed the dull-grey corrugated surface of a hand grenade. Lastly, a girl stepped off the boat, smartly dressed in a flowered cotton shift, with long dark hair streaming over her shoulders, her beautiful features betraying no hint of emotionality.

The new arrivals nodded to the American on the dock,

but no words were exchanged until they had all assembled on the veranda, leaving the helicopter pilot to tie down his craft with the help of several good-natured natives.

They sat in bamboo armchairs, and a white-coated houseboy brought round a tray of icy gin pahits. The fat man lifted his glass in silent tribute and said, 'You seem to be doing nicely for yourself, Jamieson.'

'I can't kick,' the hard-faced American replied. 'I'm the only trader in these parts, you know. I do a fair business in emeralds. Then there's the rare birds and butterflies, and a little gold gets panned in the alluvial streams inland, and an occasional trinket comes my way from the Khomar tombs. And, of course, I pick up *various other things* from time to time.'

'One is surprised at your convenient lack of competitors,' said the Arab, in flawless Lancashire English.

The American smiled without humour. 'The natives around here wouldn't allow it. I'm something of a god to them, you know.'

'I have heard something about that,' the fat man said. 'Rumour has it that you paddled in here about six years ago, more dead than alive, without a possession to your name except a pack containing five thousand doses of anti-plague serum.'

'I heard the same story,' said the Arab. 'And a week later half the population was down with bubonic.'

'Just a lucky break for me,' said the unsmiling American. 'I was right glad to be of assistance.'

'By gad, sir,' said the fat man, 'I drink to you! I do admire a man who makes his own luck.'

'What do you mean by that?' Jamieson asked.

There was a short, ominous silence. But the tension was broken by the sound of the girl laughing.

The men stared at her. Jamieson frowned and seemed

about to question her misplaced levity. Then he noticed that the English speed freak had his right hand close to the white bone handle of the long knife he carried under his shirt in a white leather pouch between his scrawny shoulder blades.

'Something itchin' you, son?' Jamieson asked, with deadly mildness.

'If there is I'll let you know,' said the boy, his blue eyes blazing. 'And my name isn't "son", it's Billy Banterville. That's who I am and who I expect to be, and anyone who says otherwise is a dirty liar and I'll be pleased to take him apart – take him apart – take him apart . . . Oh, my God, my skin is crawling off, what's happening to my skin, who lit the fuses of my nerves, why is my brain boiling? My head hurts, I need, I need.'

The fat man looked towards the Arab and nodded imperceptibly. The Arab took a hypodermic syringe from a flat, black leather case, filled it with a colourless liquid from a plastic ampoule, and deftly injected the solution into the boy's arm. Billy Banterville smiled and lay back in his chair like a jointless puppet, his pupils so enlarged that no whites could be seen, an expression of indescribable happiness upon his thin, tight face. A moment later he vanished.

'Good riddance,' said Jamieson, who had watched all of this without comment. 'Why did you bother to keep a character like that?'

'He had his uses,' said the fat man.

The girl had herself under control now. She said, 'That's it, you see. Each of us has his uses, each of us has something that is necessary to the others. You might consider us a corporate entity.'

'I see,' said Jamieson, although he didn't. 'So each of you is irreplaceable.'

'Not at all,' said the girl. 'Quite the contrary. Each of us stands in constant fear of replacement. That is why we try to stay always in each other's company – to avoid sudden and premature replacement.'

'I don't get it,' Jamieson said, although he did. He waited, but it became evident that no one was going to expatiate upon the subject. Jamieson shrugged his shoulders, suddenly ill at ease in the uncanny silence. He said, 'I suppose you'd like to get down to business?'

'If it would not be too much trouble,' said the tall Arab.

'Sure,' Jamieson said. The Arab made him feel uneasy. All of them made him feel uneasy. All except the girl. He had some ideas about her – and some plans.

Fifty yards from Jamieson's house the laboriously cleared area ended and jungle abruptly began – a green, vertical labyrinth in which a seemingly infinite number of randomly connected planes receded endlessly towards some unimaginable centre. The jungle was infinite repetition, infinite regression, infinite despair.

Standing just within the jungle margin, invisible to observers in the clearing, were two men. One was a native, a Malay to judge from his green and brown headband. He was of medium height, stocky and strongly built. His aspect was thoughtful, melancholic, tense.

His companion was a white man, tall, deeply tanned, perhaps thirty years of age, conventionally handsome, dressed in the yellow robe of a Buddhist monk. The incongruity between his appearance and his dress vanished in the fantastic contortions of the surrounding jungle.

The white man was seated cross-legged on the ground facing away from the clearing. He was in a state of extreme relaxation. His grey eyes seemed to be focused inward.

Presently the native said, 'Tuan, the man, Jamieson, has gone into his house.'

'Yes,' said the white man.

'Now he returns. He is carrying an object wrapped in burlap. It is not a large object – perhaps one-fourth the size of a young elephant's head.'

The white man did not answer.

'Now he unwraps the burlap. Within, there is an object of metal. It is of a complicated shape.'

The white man nodded.

'They have all gathered around the object,' the native went on. 'They are pleased, they are smiling. No, not all of them. The Arab has a strange expression on his face. It is not exactly displeasure. It is some emotion that I cannot describe. Yes, I can! The Arab knows something that the others don't. He is a man who thinks he has a secret advantage.'

'So much the worse for him,' the white man said. 'The others have the safety of their ignorance. That one has the peril of his understanding.'

'Do you foresee this, Tuan?'

'I read what is written,' the white man said. 'The ability to read is my curse.'

The native shuddered, fascinated and repelled. A strange pity welled up in him for this man of strange talents and great vulnerabilities.

The white man said, 'Now the fat man is holding the metal object. He gives money to Jamieson.'

'Tuan, you are not even looking at them.'

'Nevertheless, I see.'

The native shook himself like a dog. The gentle white man – his friend – had power but was himself the victim of greater power. Yes, but it was best not to think of such things, for the white man's destiny was not his destiny, and he thanked his God for that.

'Now they are going inside Jamieson's house,' the native said. 'But you know that, do you not, Tuan?'

'I know. I am unable not to know.'

'And you know what they are doing within the house?'

'This, too, I cannot avoid.'

The native said, impulsively, 'Tell me only what I must hear.'

'That is all I ever tell you,' the white man said. Then, without looking at the native, he said, 'You should leave me, leave this place. You should go to another island, get a wife, go into business.'

'No, Tuan. We are yoked together, you and I. There is no avoiding it. As you know.'

'Yes, I know. But sometimes I hope I am wrong, just for once. I would give a great deal to be wrong.'

'It is not in your nature.'

'Perhaps not. Still, I can hope.' The white man shrugged. 'Now the fat man has put the metal object into a black leather satchel. They are all smiling and shaking hands and there is murder in the air. Come, let us go away now.'

'Is there not a chance they will escape us?'

'It no longer matters. The ending is wrought in iron. We will go away and eat now and then sleep.'

'And then?'

The white man shook his head wearily. 'You do not need to know that. Come.'

They moved into the jungle. The native prowled with the silent grace of a tiger. The white man drifted like a ghost.

70

Less than a mile from Jamieson's house, down a narrow path hacked through the jungle, one came to the native settlement of Omandrik. At first glance this was a typical Tamili village, identical to a hundred others that could be found perched precariously along the banks of the Semil River – that lost brown stream that seemed barely to have the energy to flow through the devouring sunburned country to the distant, shallow, reef-strewn waters of the East Java Sea.

But an observant eye, ranging across the village, would take in the small, unmistakable signs of neglect – thatch blown away on many of the huts, taro patches overgrown with weeds, broken-hulled praus scattered along the river-bank. One also noticed indistinct black shapes scurrying between huts – an infestation of rats grown bold enough to raid the forlorn gardens in daylight. This more than any other single thing demonstrated the apathy of the villagers, their weary state of demoralization. A proverb of the coast asserts that the presence of rats in daylight means that the land is abandoned of the gods.

In the centre of the village, in a hut nearly twice the size of the others, Amhdi, the headman, sat cross-legged in front of a battery-operated shortwave radio. The radio gave off a low hiss of static, and its green signal indicator glowed like a panther's eye caught in a moonbeam. This was all the radio was capable of, since it had lost its antenna long before old Amhdi had acquired it. But the static and the wavering green light were marvels enough for the old man. The radio had become his spiritual counsellor. He consulted it every few days and declared that the spirits of the dead whispered advice to him and that the spirit eye revealed marvels that could not be revealed.

Tanine, his priest, had never been able to determine whether the old chief actually believed this nonsense or whether he used the 'magic' radio out of a previously unsuspected depth of guile to escape some of the more onerous mandates of the House of the Knife. Standing near the old chief, arms folded, clad in a sombre pegatu with the sacred monkey's skull fastened to his high forehead, the priest decided that the chief's deception was largely unconscious: a will to escape domination and a will to believe neatly conjoined. Nor could the priest blame his headman, whatever his motive: the years had not been kind to Amhdi, and the House of the Knife had been unable to alleviate his sufferings. The old man's attitude was understandable, not that that would stop the priest from doing what he had to do, for an adept of the Snake-Redeemer had certain duties to fulfil no matter what violence they might do to his own emotions.

'Well, Chief?' the priest asked.

The old man looked up furtively. He turned off the radio; it was difficult to obtain batteries – the precious spirit food – from the violent trader in the big house by the river bend. Besides, he had heard the message, the thin voice of his father, nearly lost in the whispering of a thousand other spirits, pleading, cursing, promising, seeking communication with the living from their black house at the end of the world.

'My wise ancient one has spoken to me,' Amhdi said. Never had he referred to his father by name or by relationship.

'And what did he say, O Chief?' the priest asked, no hint of irony evident in the low, controlled voice.

'He has told me what must be done about the strangers.'

The priest nodded slowly: This was unusual. The headman detested making decisions, and his spirit voices usually advised him along the comfortable rut of inaction. So the old man was beginning to assert himself? Or could it be that his father, the legendary warrior ... No, it could not be. It simply could not be.

The priest waited for his chief to tell him what the wise ancient one had advised about the strangers. But Amhdi seemed reluctant to talk. Perhaps he had sensed that he had gained a momentary advantage in a contest that the priest had thought long resolved. Nothing could be read on the old man's face except its customary expression of baffled avarice and weak guile.

71

The Man of a Thousand Disguises stirred uneasily, almost awoke, almost recognized himselves.

OUT FOR A SWIM IN THE COLLECTIVE POOL OF THE UNCONSCIOUS

'Name?'
'Proteus.'
'Occupation?'
'Shape-changer.'
'Sex?'

'Any.'
'Brocade?'
'Nexus.'

Perseverance brings sublime success. Despite the pain, proceed by contiguities. Premature closure is false healing. Do not anticipate.

All movement is a search, all expectation is of failure, all searches find completion in their origins. The entire pattern is implicit in the first stitch; the initial brushstroke is the ultimate ornament. But this is forbidden knowledge, since the entire dance must be danced.

Initial movement is always initiation.

Mishkin's presence must be inferred by his absence. Mishkin's engine part is found. All that remains is to find it.

DO NOT CUT ALONG THE LINE

The port of Arachnis is situated on a misshapen arm of land extending into the sun-shattered waters of the East Java Sea. It is a typical South Asian city compounded of chaos, and intershot with strict and inexplicable rules of behaviour. The scent of a hundred mingled and exotic spices perturbs the senses of the voyager while he is still many miles at sea. These odours, in their ever-changing combinations, touch hidden sensations in the Westerner that are incalculable in their effect. Memories are elicited of events never experienced by the individual; absurd and impossible sensations are stirred. This sensory onslaught cannot fail to have its impact upon the voyager accustomed to the tepid reception afforded by the bland cities of the West. Effortlessly, the East penetrates the outer, rational, prosaic surface of the voyager's personality, shaping and changing him, subjecting him to fragments of vision, moments of horror and illumination, to inimitable languors and abrupt passions. The approach to Arachnis is the first step into a dream.

Of course, all of this is unacknowledged by the sturdy Western traveller. It was not even considered by the two men and a woman who, at sunset, sailed their steam launch into the crescent-shaped inner harbour of Arachnis. Their ignorance was childish and touching, but it was no defence against the unthinkable world that was engulfing them.

They docked in gathering darkness. Their plans had long been made. Provision had been made for everything, for all the anticipated permutations of chance. Everything had been calculated except the incalculable.

The Arab and the girl stayed on the boat and guarded the object in the burlap bag. The fat man left the boat and walked away from the harbour into the walled city, past the Street of Bird Sellers, the Street of Dogs, the Street of Forgetfulness, the Street of Many Doors ... Droll, the names they had, if one was in the mood for that sort of thing.

The fat man did not feel well. The motion of the boat had given him a queasiness that had not yet passed. His system had been subjected to various shocks, and he was not a man to adapt easily.

Still, the work was nearly finished. It was amusing to remember how it had begun. An elderly man had contacted him. The elderly man wanted a certain object – an engine part – delivered to a certain man, a relative, marooned on a planet called Harmonia, unable to return until he received the part for his disabled spaceship. The problem had seemed straightforward enough – a simple matter of logistics. But there had been unforeseen complications, which had mounted until finally there seemed no way of delivering the engine part – not until the young relative became an old man or a dead man. Therefore, businessman that he was, the elderly gentleman had looked into other channels. And he had come upon the fat man.

That, at least, was his story. It was as good as any other story, and almost as likely.

And now the thing was nearly done. Already the fat man had put behind him the unresolved complications he had encountered while dealing with Jamieson, and by extension, with the local chief, his priest, and the mysterious white man in the jungle. Everybody was mysterious until you knew their motivations (every situation was complicated as long as you stayed within its frame of reference). But people didn't realize that a man could walk away, simply leave a situation unresolved, its riddles unanswered. It required will power to do that and even more will power not to pursue unproductive questions such as: How had the engine part come to that unlikely village in southern Asia; Who was the white man in the jungle and why was he so interested in the part; Why had the chief come to a decision now, after years of indecision; Why had Jamieson, a shrewd trader, let the engine part go for so small a price; Why had no one interfered with the fat man and his helpers during their departure? And so on and so on, *ad infinitum.*

But the fat man had resisted the commonplace traps baited

with curiosity. He knew that mystery is only a lack of data and that for all questions there are only a small number of answers, infinitely repeated, typically banal. Curiosity kills. One simply had to leave behind all the enticing problems, the delicious irrationalities, and move on at the proper time – as he had done.

Everything was going very well indeed. The fat man was pleased. He only wished that the nagging hollowness in his stomach would pass. That and the vertigo.

The Street of Monkeys, the Street of Twilight, the Street of Memory. What strange names these people chose! Or had the Tourist Board done the inventing? It didn't matter, he had memorized his route long ago, he knew exactly how to proceed. He walked without haste through the bazaar, past stacks of swords, baskets of green and orange nuts, piles of fat, silvery fish, past cotton cloth dyed the colours of the rainbow, past a group of grinning black men beating on drums while a golden youth performed a dance, past jugglers and fire-eaters, past a man who sat quietly holding a gorilla on a leash.

The heat was unusual even for the tropics, as were the smells – of spices, kerosene, charcoal, cooking oil, dung – and the sounds – chattering alien voices, squeak of a water wheel, groaning of cattle, high-pitched bark of dogs, jingle of brass jewellery.

There were other sounds, not to be identified: other scenes, not to be understood or assimilated. A man in a black headband was making a slow, deep incision in a boy's thigh with an inlaid shell knife while a crowd watched and giggled. Five men solemnly pounded their fists against a strip of corrugated iron, the blood running down their arms. There was a man with a blue stone in his turban that gave off wisps of white smoke.

And yet overall there remained that sense of vertigo that made everything turn and fall slowly to the left – and the hollowness, as if he had lost something large and intimate from within him. Business was not much fun when you were unwell : see a doctor in Singapore next week, meanwhile walk past the Street of Thieves, Street of Deaths, Street of Forgetfulness – damn their pretentiousness – down the Street of the Maze, Street of Desire, Street of Fish, Fulfilment, Nuts, Two Demons, Horses, and only a few more blocks to Ahlid's house.

A beggar clutched at his sleeve. 'The smallest coin, compassionate one, that I may live one more day.'

'I never give to beggars,' the fat man said.

'Never at all?'

'No. It is a matter of principle.'

'Then take this,' the beggar said, and pressed into the fat man's hand a shrivelled fig.

'Why do you give this to me?' asked the fat man.

'A matter of caprice. I am too poor to afford principles.'

The fat man moved on, holding the fig, unwilling to drop it while the beggar could still see him, his head spinning now, his legs beginning to tremble.

He came to a fortune-telling booth. An aged crone blocked his way.

'Learn your fortune, great sir! Learn what will become of you!'

'I never have my fortune told,' the fat man said. 'A matter of principle.' But then he remembered the beggar. 'Besides, I cannot afford it.'

'You have the price in your hand!' the crone said. She took the fig from him and led him to her booth. She took a bronze jar and spilled its contents on to the counter. In the jar there were twenty or thirty coins of many shapes, sizes, and colours. She studied them intently and looked at the fat man.

'I see change and becoming,' she said. 'I see resistance, then yielding, then defeat, then victory. I see completion and beginning again.'

'Can't you be more specific?' asked the fat man. His forehead and cheeks were burning. His throat was dry and it was painful to swallow.

'Of course, I can,' the old woman said. 'But I won't, since compassion is a virtue and you are an attractive man.'

She turned away abruptly. The fat man picked up a small coin of hammered iron from the counter and walked away.

Street of Initiation, Street of Ivory.

A woman stopped him. She was neither young nor old. She had strong features, dark eyes rimmed with kohl, lips painted with ochre. 'My darling,' she said, 'my full moon, my palm tree! The price is cheap, the pleasure is unforgettable.'

'I think not,' the fat man said.

'Think of the pleasure, my beloved, the pleasure!'

And, strangely, the fat man knew that he would enjoy this dirty, diseased woman of the streets, enjoy her more than the predictable and sterile couplings he had experienced in the past. Onset of romanticism! But it was out of the question, syphilis was rampant in this place, he didn't have the time, he couldn't stop now.

'Some other time,' he said.

'Alas! That will never be!'

'You can never tell.'

She looked boldly into his eyes. 'Sometimes you can tell. It will never be.'

'Take this to remember me by,' the fat man said and pushed the iron coin into her hand.

'It is wise of you to pay,' she said. 'Soon you will see what you have bought.'

The fat man turned away and continued to walk mechanically. His joints ached. Definitely, he was not well. Street of the Razor, Street of the End, and now he had come to the house of the merchant Ahlid.

73

The fat man knocked at the great brass-studded door of Ahlid's house. A servant let him in and took him through an inner courtyard to a cool, dim, high-ceilinged room. The fat man felt relieved to sit on soft brocaded cushions and to sip iced mint tea from a frosted silver glass. But he still felt strange and out of sorts, and the vertigo had not left him. His condition annoyed him. It was most inconvenient.

Ahlid entered the room, a quiet, slender man in his fifties. The fat man had saved his life during a time of riots in Mukhtail. Ahlid had been grateful, and more important, reliable. They had done business together in Aden, Port Sudan, and Karachi. They had not met since Ahlid had moved to Arachnis some years ago.

Ahlid inquired about the fat man's health and listened with grave concern to his indispositions.

'It seems that I cannot take this climate,' the fat man said. 'But it is of no concern. How are you, my friend, and how is your wife and child?'

'I am well enough,' said Ahlid. 'Despite the unsettled times, I manage to earn a sufficient living. My wife died two years ago of a snakebite suffered in the bazaar. My daughter is well enough; later you will meet her.'

The fat man murmured his regrets. Ahlid thanked him and said, 'One learns how to live with Death in this city. Death is present everywhere in the world, of course, and in due time takes everyone; but in other cities he is less publicly evident. Elsewhere, Death makes his customary rounds of the hospitals, goes for a drive on the highway, takes a stroll around town to visit the needy, and generally comports himself like a respectable citizen. To be sure, he arranges a few surprises now and again; but in general he does his work as expected and tries not to disrupt the reasonable hopes and expectations of sober and respectable men.

'But here in Arachnis, Death behaves in quite a different way. Perhaps he is affected by the fierce sun and the marshy land, perhaps they are responsible for making him moody, capricious, and unrelenting. Whatever the causes, Death is ubiquitous and unexpected here, taking delight in sudden surprises and reversals, visiting all parts of the city, not even respecting the mosques and palaces where a man might expect some small measure of security. Here, Death is no longer a good citizen. Here he is a cheap dramatist.'

'I beg your pardon,' the fat man said. 'I seem to have dozed off. The heat ... What have we been talking about?'

'You had inquired about my daughter,' said Ahlid. 'She is seventeen years old. Perhaps you would like to meet her now?'

'Delighted, delighted,' said the fat man.

Ahlid led him through dark corridors, up a wide staircase, then through a gallery whose narrow, slit windows looked down upon an interior patio with a fountain. They came to a door. Ahlid knocked, and opened it.

The room was brilliantly lighted. The floor was of black

marble, into which a great number of white lines had been let. The lines crossed and recrossed each other at irregular intervals like a tangle of twine. In the centre of the room sat a grave, dark-eyed girl, dressed in white, stitching on a little embroidery frame.

'Charming,' said the fat man. The girl did not look up. The tip of her tongue stood out as she concentrated on her design. The pattern of her embroidery was poorly executed, chaotic.

'She is docile,' said Ahlid.

The fat man rubbed his eyes. With an effort he sat upright in his chair. He was in Ahlid's salon again, seated on brocade cushions. Ahlid was writing in an account book. In front of the fat man there was a half-eaten cup of sherbet.

The fat man said, 'Please excuse my lapses. I have not been well. Perhaps it would be best if we discussed business.'

'Just as you please,' Ahlid said.

'I have come here,' the fat man said, 'to arrange, with your help, and at a mutually agreeable price, to . . . I have a certain object in my possession, of no intrinsic importance except to the man who . . . I wish to transport a certain engine part to a certain place, and I am confident that I, or rather, you, can accomplish . . . I seem to be having difficulty in expressing myself. This thing that I wish to accomplish . . .'

'My friend,' said Ahlid, 'isn't it time that we talked seriously?'

'Yes? I can assure you . . .'

'Isn't it time that we talked about what you would like to do with the little time remaining to you?' Ahlid asked.

The fat man managed to smile. 'I will admit that I am indisposed. But no one can know . . .'

'Please,' said Ahlid. 'My friend, my benefactor, I am very sorry to have to tell you that you have the plague.'

'Plague? Don't be ridiculous. I grant that I am not well. I will consult a doctor.'

'I have already summoned my own doctor,' Ahlid said. 'But I know the signs of the plague well. All of us in Arachnis know it, for plague is entwined throughout our lives.'

'That is quite incredible,' said the fat man.

'Why would I deceive you?' Ahlid said. 'I tell you this because I am sure of it. Must you waste your valuable time denying it?'

The fat man sat silently for a long time. Then he said, dully, 'I knew when I came ashore here that I was seriously ill. Ahlid, how long do I have?'

'Perhaps three weeks, perhaps a month, even two.'

'No more than that?'

'No more.'

'I see,' said the fat man. 'Well, then ... Is there a hospital here?'

'None worthy of the name. You will stay here with me.'

'Out of the question,' said the fat man. 'The risk of contagion ...'

'No one escapes contagion in Arachnis,' Ahlid said. 'Listen to me: you have come home to live a little while and then die. This is your home, I am your family.'

The fat man smiled vaguely and shook his head.

'You do not understand,' Ahlid said. 'Death is a part of life. Therefore, there can be no rejection of it. What cannot be rejected must be accepted. What we cannot overcome we must submit to. And since we are men, our submission must be as strong as our rejection. You are very fortunate that you have been granted this chance to prepare yourself for Death and to do so here, in a cool and pleasant house – in your own house. It is not a bad thing.'

'No, it is not,' said the fat man. 'But it will be a depressing time for you.'

'Your death will not depress me any more than will my own,' said Ahlid. 'You and I will talk together in the days ahead. You will make your preparations. And you will help me.'

'How?'

'My acceptance of my own death is still very imperfect,' said Ahlid. 'Through you, I hope to learn what you must learn : how to submit strongly.'

'And your daughter?'

'The thread of her life is slender. Surely, you have noticed that? She also must learn.'

'Very well,' the fat man said. 'It is all very strange, and yet it is not strange at all . . . I am at the moment less startled by the imminence of my death than by the fact that you have become a philosopher.'

Ahlid shook his head. 'I am a worldly man and a frightened man. But I am a man. I will look at what is in front of me.'

'And I, too,' said the fat man. 'It has taken us many years to pay attention to what is important.'

'That is not strange at all,' Ahlid said. 'If all men paid due attention to the great and important questions who would be left to make iced sherbet?'

'You are right again,' said the fat man. 'Now I would like to lie down for a while. Then we will talk more.'

Ahlid rang a bell. 'The servant and I will assist you to your bedroom. The doctor will be here before you awaken. He cannot cure you, but he can ease pain. Do you wish me to do anything about the business you were talking about?'

'No,' said the fat man. 'I don't care about that any more.'

'Then we will speak of it no more. In one way or another, business matters always seem to solve themselves.'

The servant came, and the fat man was helped to a cool white bedroom. He realized that he was happy. Truly, nothing upon the earth could be predicted.

Mishkin sat at his desk at the foot of the glass mountain that lay just beyond the great forest of Harmonia. He drank his morning coffee. The robot brought in the day's mail.

First there was an official government notice concerning the undeliverability of Engine Part L-1223A. Five reasons were listed. Mishkin didn't bother to read them. The government notice was mimeographed.

Next, there was a letter from Uncle Arnold:

Dear Tom, You should only know the things I've done and the wires I've pulled, but nothing works, I just can't seem to get that engine part to you. I haven't given up hope, however. (Your Uncle Arnie never gives up hope!) Maybe you didn't know that your second nephew, Irving Gluckman, is a consulting accountant for a branch of the Rand Corporation. I'm going to ask him to ask his boss if they'll take on your problem as a matter of affecting the National Interest, which, in a way, it is. All of this may take a little time, so if you can get home in any other way it might be a good idea to do just that. Keep your chin up, and my best regards to your robot.

Finally, there was a letter from The Man of a Thousand Disguises:

Dear Tom, I've tried everything in my power, and quite a few things beyond my power, to send you that engine part and get you out of this unfortunate mess, which I take full responsibility for getting you into. I even went so far as to construct an entire new sequence, with impeccable supporting logic and character relationships, all for the sole purpose of delivering the engine part to you. But my main (new) character caught the plague, lost all interest in life, and summarily refused to complete the job I had created him for. I tried to get his two helpers to do it, but they had fallen in love and gone off to the Seychelles Islands to make jewellery and live on organic foods. So I spent a hell of a lot of time and wordage to no purpose whatsoever, and I really am sorry, but that was my last bright idea, and now my doctor tells me that I must take a rest.

Tom, forgive me, my nerves are shot, I'm broke, and there's simply nothing more I can do for you. I can't tell you how sorry I am that it has all worked out this way, especially since you've been so helpful and patient right from the beginning.

I am enclosing under separate cover a box of Hershey bars with almonds, a tortilla press, and a manuscript copy of my newest book, entitled *How to Survive on an Alien Planet.* According to impartial readers, this is a well-researched and hiply written examination of problems very similar to yours and contains many practical hints and suggestions. Stay well, old buddy, keep the old flag flying and all that sort of thing. If anything turns up I'll act immediately, but you really shouldn't count on it.

All the best –
The Author

75 Black Moment

Ah, the loneliness of it all! The abandonment! The pain! Quick, Watson, the needle, the pill, the joint, the pellet! Too many stars, too many stares. Disembody. But first eat the nice cream cheese and jelly sandwich.

76 Final Transformation

'Tommy! Stop playing now!'

'I'm not playing, Mom. This is *real*.'

'I know. But you have to stop playing now and come home.'

Mishkin laughed bitterly. 'I can't *get* home, that's the whole problem. I need a part for my spaceship . . .'

'I *told* you to stop playing. Put down that broom and come into the house at once.'

'It's not a broom, it's a spaceship. Anyhow, my robot says . . .'

'And bring that old radio in with you. Come in right now and eat your dinner.'

'Right *now*, Mom? Can't I play a little longer?'

'It's almost dark, and you have homework to do. Come inside right now.'

'Aw . . .'

'And kindly do not sulk.'

'All right. But *really*, it is a spaceship, and it is broken.'
'All right, it's a broken spaceship. Are you coming in?'
'Yes, Mom, I'm coming in right now.'

77 Final Deformations

The Man of a Thousand Disguises turns into Mishkin. The robot changes into Uncle Arnold, who turns into Orchidius, who changes into the fat man, who turns into the robot, who changes into The Man of a Thousand Disguises, who changes into Mishkin, who changes . . . coalesces, combines.

There will be a short intermission while the appearances reindividualize themselves. Music of the spheres will be played. Refreshments will be served. Insights will be projected by the Illusion Machine. Smoking is permitted.

FINAL EXHIBIT

A photograph of the 2nd battalion of the 32nd infantry regiment, 7th division, 8th Army. It is a long photograph, a scroll, a souvenir. Unroll it carefully. How much alike the faces are! But look – Mishkin is in the fourth row from the bottom, third face from the left. He has a silly smirk on his face. He is in no way remarkable.

Other Pan books that may interest you are listed on the following pages

Robert Sheckley
The People Trap 60p

In these fourteen highly imaginative tales the master works his usual magic. This long-awaited collection has a basic theme: escape from an outrageous situation either on an alien planet or on a satirically visualized future on Earth.

'Excellent . . . does not hide an awful warning of the urban chaos and anarchy that may be nearer than we think'
YORKSHIRE POST

The Same to You Doubled 35p

The resourceful vacuum cleaner that falls in love with a suburban wife . . .

A mechanical perimeter guard that nearly kills its controller . . .

The mild-mannered man who, thanks to the god Thoth-Hermes, need never again be pushed around by authority. . .

A quintessential collection of sixteen tales to delight and intrigue every SF enthusiast. The time is in the future and the rules of logic are thrown to the wind.

'From the man with the most way-out sense of humour in SF. He can make the most frightening situation seem hilarious and this selection is no exception'
YORKSHIRE POST.

Mindswap 35p

'Gentleman from Mars, age 43, quiet, studious, cultured, wishes to exchange bodies with similarly inclined Earth gentleman; August 1 – September 1. References exchanged. Brokers. Protected.'

Exchanging bodies for touristic purposes having become commonplace, Marvin Flynn books a trip to Mars. Once there the unexpected happens and Marvin's mind must seek refuge in a series of temporary bodies on different planets – with some very surprising results . . .

Arthur C. Clarke
Rendezvous with Rama 60p

Rama – a metallic cylinder approaching the Sun at a tremendous velocity. Rama – first product of an alien civilization to be encountered by man. Rama – a world of technological marvels and artificial ecology. What is its purpose in this year 2131? Who is inside it? And why?

Childhood's End 60p

Blotting out the light from the stars they had linked so effortlessly, the silent ships hang suspended over the great cities of Earth . . . Armed with a staggering power and an infinite wisdom, the invaders from outer space shock Earth into submission – but what is their purpose?

A Fall of Moondust 60p

The setting – Moon in the 21st century – is depicted vividly and convincingly. But the vital core of the novel is this: will the crew and passengers of the Dust-cruiser *Selene*, buried fifteen metres down in the Sea of Thirst, be rescued before several possible catastrophes overcome them?

The Deep Range 60p

After a terrifying nightmare in outer space, Walter Franklin needs to discover a reason for living, and he finds it in the ocean depths, where strangers defy death to give him life. But Franklin is haunted by the memory of an echo, an echo that could solve the oldest mystery of the Sun.

Also available
Earthlight 50p
Profiles of the Future 70p